A Haunted Invitation

A LIN COFFIN

COZY MYSTERY

BOOK 5

J.A. WHITING

COPYRIGHT 2016 J.A. WHITING

Cover copyright 2016 Signifer Book Design

Formatting by Signifer Book Design

Proofreading by Donna Rich

This book is a work of fiction. Names, characters, places, or incidents are products of the author's imagination or are used fictitiously. Any resemblance to locales, actual events, or persons, living or dead, is entirely coincidental.

All rights reserved.

No part of this publication can be reproduced or transmitted in any form or by any means, electronic or mechanical, without permission in writing from J. A. Whiting.

To hear about new books and book sales, please sign up for my mailing list at: www.jawhitingbooks.com

For my family, with love

A Haunted Invitation

CHAPTER 1

Lin Coffin had been sitting at the deck table with her boyfriend, Jeff, for over two hours talking under a jet black sky dotted with sparkling stars. The flickering candle in a glass jar on the center of the table had almost burned down to a stub when the chill night air caused the two young people to shiver and decide to move into Lin's living room.

The conversation that the two had been having was a serious one and Lin's stomach had felt like a clenched fist for the entire first hour of their talk. What she had to tell her boyfriend was so unusual that she braced herself for rejection. She had only told two other people her secret, one a young girl she'd thought was her friend who ended up blabbing the news to their entire elementary school causing Lin a terrible year of teasing and bullying. The other person was her cousin, Viv, who took the news with awe and interest and accepted it as a fascinating facet of who her cousin was.

Lin wondered which way Jeff would lean after hearing about his girlfriend's special "skill." Since before she could talk, Lin Coffin could see ghosts.

"Let's go inside." Jeff stood up and reached for Lin's hand.

Lin wiped her clammy hand on her jeans before placing it in Jeff's. "My hands have been sweating the entire time we've been talking."

Jeff smiled and wrapped Lin in his arms. "I wouldn't be much of a boyfriend if I couldn't accept your, ah ... ability." Jeff had listened intently to Lin's experiences and he sprinkled her telling with an occasional thoughtful question.

He led her from the deck to the small sofa in the living room of her Nantucket cottage where they continued their chat sitting close together, side by side. It would have been a romantic setting except that Lin's little brown dog, Nicky, had wedged himself between them.

"Gee, Nick," Jeff said to the friendly creature as he placed his arm over Lin's shoulders. "Who needs a chaperone with you around?"

The dog wagged his tail and licked Jeff's cheek.

After another hour of talk and questions, Jeff sat pensively for several minutes.

"Do you have more things you'd like to ask?" Lin squeezed his hand. "It's okay. You can ask me anything you want."

"It's not that." Jeff had a puzzled or confused expression on his face that Lin couldn't read.

"You know that job I've been working on recently? I'm doing finish work at the old mansion

A Haunted Invitation

that my buddy, Kurt's, construction company has been renovating."

Lin nodded and looked at Jeff with interest.

"The woman who owns the house, the other day she told me something while I was working. I blew it off at the time. Now, I don't know."

"What was it that she said?" Lin wondered if her revelation about ghosts had something to do with Jeff's comments.

"It was odd." Jeff smiled, but then when he looked at Lin, his smile faded. "She didn't say too much, but now that I think of it, my reaction probably squashed her interest in telling me more."

Lin cocked her head waiting for her boyfriend to reveal what the woman told him.

Jeff ran his hand through his hair and shook his head. "I was dumb. I kind of chuckled when she talked about what she'd seen. I shouldn't have done that. I feel really bad about it now."

"Jeff." Lin was getting impatient. She gave him a playful poke in the side. "What are you going on about? Tell me what she said."

Jeff hugged Lin's shoulders. "Sorry. The whole thing is running through my head now because of what we've been discussing. The woman who owns the house I was working on, her name's Mrs. Perkins, she came in to see the changes and updates that are being made to the place. She's been staying in a house that's three doors up from the one we're working on. She owns both places. Mrs. Perkins is staying in the other house while the construction's going on. The house is right near the Founders Inn and Restaurant."

While listening to Jeff, Lin ran her hand over Nicky's soft brown fur.

"So while I was working, she struck up a conversation with me. She asked about my experience, if I was born on-island, do I work on a lot of old houses, things like that. We were having a pleasant chat although I have to admit that I was a little distracted from the discussion because I was focusing so keenly on making the proper cuts and fittings."

"What bothers you about what she said to you?"

"She told me about something that happened in the neighborhood and then she asked me if I believed in ghosts. She asked in a joking sort of way."

"What did you say?"

"I chuckled and told her that many people claim that lots of houses on the island are haunted."

Lin winced at the word.

"Did I say something wrong?" Jeff asked when he saw Lin's reaction.

"No, not really. I've just never liked the word 'haunted.' It probably stems from being teased as a kid."

"What should I use instead?"

Lin smiled at Jeff and her heart warmed at his thoughtfulness in wanting to use the vocabulary that she preferred when talking about spirits. "Use whatever suits the situation. It's okay."

"So, Mrs. Perkins asked me if I'd ever seen a ghost." Jeff sighed. "I told her no, but you know what? I think I did see one once when I was really little."

Lin nearly jumped out of her skin. "What? You did?" The excitement in her voice caused Nicky to lift his head and woof. "It's okay, Nick." Lin looked at Jeff. "You saw a ghost?"

"Well, it was only the one time. I never saw anything like it again. My sister, Dana, and I were playing in her room. It was probably midnight and we were supposed to be asleep. I was little, maybe three or four years old. I felt chilly and looked up to see a man dressed in old-fashioned clothes sitting in the rocker by the door. He was just watching us play. He gave me a kind smile. Dana looked up and waved at him."

"Dana could see him, too?" Lin stared at her boyfriend. Never in a million years would she have thought that Jeff and his sister had an experience with ghosts.

Jeff nodded. "We went back to playing. When I looked up again, the man was gone. Neither of us felt threatened or frightened. We thought nothing of it. It seemed fine to have the man there. We mentioned it the next morning at breakfast. Our mom stared at us. I remember it distinctly, the expression on her face. She wasn't pleased. I almost felt like we had done something wrong. My mom told us that there's no such thing as ghosts and she turned away." Jeff gave a shrug. "I never saw a spirit or a ghost or anything like that ever again. I haven't even brought it up with Dana since that day. Odd, huh?"

Lin shook her head. "I've read that lots of little kids can see ghosts, but the reaction from whoever they tell is often negative so they stop seeing them."

"*You* didn't stop though." Jeff's facial expression was pensive as he tried to understand why Lin continued to see spirits even though she had been bullied about it as a kid at school.

"I guess my ability is stronger than most people's. After being teased at school, I didn't want to see spirits ever again and they left me alone for twenty years. It's when I came back to Nantucket that they started making appearances again." Lin sighed. Sometimes she wished the ghosts would just leave her alone, but then she'd feel guilty for thinking that way because sometimes they needed her help … and Lin was determined to use her skill to make things better.

"Why do you think they started to show themselves again?" Jeff asked.

"Maybe because they think I can handle it now that I'm older?" Lin rubbed her finger over her heirloom horseshoe necklace that once belonged to an ancestor who could also see spirits.

"That could be." Jeff gave a shrug of his

A Haunted Invitation

shoulder. "Funny, I hadn't thought of seeing that ghost-man for ages." He smiled at Lin. "I guess if you live on the island, you will most likely encounter a spirit at some time or another." Nantucket had a reputation as a place with many ghosts and apparitions.

Lin took Jeff's hand. "When Mrs. Perkins talked to you, did she mention actually seeing a ghost?"

"She didn't come out and say it, but I think that's what she was hinting at. Maybe I'm wrong and I'm misinterpreting the whole thing." Jeff frowned. "Now I feel really bad for being so glib about it with her." He pushed himself straighter on the sofa. "Mrs. Perkins told me about a strange experience she had a couple of days ago. She said that the other night she woke up from a sound sleep and heard noises outside her window. She got up and looked out. There was a group of men moving heavy cartons out of the back door of the restaurant at the Founders Inn that's near her house. Mrs. Perkins could see the men from the second floor bedroom window." Jeff looked at Lin. "Mrs. Perkins told me that there was something about the way those men looked. She said they just didn't look right."

"How did she mean?"

"I thought she meant they looked drunk. Now, I think she might have meant something else."

"What happened then? Did the workers go away?"

"Mrs. Perkins said the noise went on for two hours with the men shouting and laughing and dragging heavy containers over the dirt of the back lot. She was so annoyed that she called the police."

Lin wanted to ask a million questions, but she resisted.

"Just before the police arrived, the men hid in a gulley next to the restaurant's rear lot. Mrs. Perkins said the police got out, swiped their flashlights over the lot, and then got back in their cruiser and drove away."

"Was that the end of it?"

"No. She said the men came back and started the whole thing up again. Mrs. Perkins watched them until dawn. This is the part that got me thinking. She said that she felt *transfixed* by the goings-on. She thought about calling the police again, but she couldn't bother to move away from the window."

"Huh. Did the men just drive off then when morning came?" Lin asked.

"Mrs. Perkins wasn't sure. She had fallen asleep. She said she woke up mid-morning on the floor next to the window."

Lin blinked. "How very odd."

"While she was telling me this, one of the other workers called Mrs. Perkins into another room. As she walked away, she muttered again that those men just didn't look right. It kind of gave me a chill."

A Haunted Invitation

Lin gave a nod and took in a deep breath. *I bet those men didn't look right because they're dead.*

CHAPTER 2

Lin and Viv sat hunched forward at a table in the back of the bookstore café. Viv had taken a few minutes from the morning rush to hear what had gone on when Lin talked to Jeff the previous night. "I can't believe it. I can't believe you told him." Viv's blue eyes were like saucers. "Once you decided to tell Jeff about your, um … skill, I thought you'd worry over it for weeks before you actually talked to him about it."

"It was a spur of the moment decision. I was tired of hiding it from him. It just seemed like the right time to do it." Lin was dressed in jean shorts, a tank top, and work boots. She'd stopped into Viv's bookstore before heading off to her landscaping jobs to tell her cousin in person that she'd revealed to Jeff her ability to see the ghosts. "I was a nervous wreck. Just thinking about it now makes me start to sweat. When I started to tell him, I felt dizzy, almost like I was about to faint, but I couldn't stop once I started the conversation."

"Well, right." Viv nodded. "You can't start a

A Haunted Invitation

discussion by saying 'Oh, by the way, I can see ghosts' and then change your mind about talking about it." Viv leaned forward. "Wow, I can't believe how well he took it. It's a relief, isn't it?"

"It sure is." Lin fiddled with the ends of her long, brown ponytail. "Jeff mentioned that there are lots of reports of ghosts on the island and more people than we suspect have probably come across a spirit at least once in their life. He's right, I bet."

Viv pouted, feeling left out. "I haven't seen one. Ever. And I've lived on-island almost my whole life. And I have Coffin and Witchard ancestors, too." Both cousins were descended from some of Nantucket's early founders, and some of those ancestors had special "skills."

"Give it time." Lin smiled. "You're bound to run into a ghost eventually."

Nicky sat with Viv's gray cat, Queenie, in an upholstered chair off to the side. He looked over at Viv and gave a happy little yip.

"Nicky agrees." Lin glanced around the café. "Do you have a few more minutes? I want to tell you something that Jeff told me last night."

Viv turned her head and raised her index finger to indicate to her employee, Mallory, that she'd be back to work the beverage counter in a few minutes. "Make it fast or Mallory will have my head."

Lin told her cousin about the men who Mrs. Perkins recently saw working all night long at the back of the inn-restaurant, how the police came by but didn't stay long, and how the woman felt transfixed by the late-night activity. "And," Lin narrowed her eyes. "Mrs. Perkins mentioned several times that the men just didn't look right."

"What's that supposed to mean? They didn't look right?" Viv took a quick look over to the customers queuing in front of the counter and then turned back to her cousin.

When Lin paused for several moments, Viv's eyebrows shot up. "What are you thinking?"

"I think those men are dead."

Viv sucked in a fast breath. She still wasn't used to ghosts and spirits and apparitions invading her life via her cousin. "Oh, no. Really? There must be another explanation." She eyed Lin. "Don't you think?"

Lin gave a slight shrug of one shoulder.

Viv swallowed. "Well, maybe they'll go away. It doesn't involve you. You're not the one who saw them."

Lin leveled her eyes at her cousin. She knew full well that something involving those men was going to demand her attention. She could feel it.

"Oh, no." Viv nervously pushed a lock of hair from her eyes. "What's this going to be about? Let's talk about it later. I need to get back to work." Standing up, she hugged Lin. "Whatever it is, we'll deal with it. At least Jeff knows now." Heading over to take her place at the beverage counter, Viv looked back. "And he didn't break off with you over

A Haunted Invitation

it either."

Lin smiled at her cousin and as she popped the last bite of her chocolate croissant into her mouth, she sensed someone approaching her table. She turned to see Jeff's friend, Kurt, walking towards her carrying a take-out coffee cup. "Hey, Lin."

Lin was still chewing her pastry and could only smile and nod.

"Have you talked to Jeff this morning?" Kurt owned a construction and renovation business and Jeff was often hired to help out on the different projects. "I asked him to talk to you about doing a bit of landscaping at the house we're renovating. It's a small yard. It's just the front and side of the house that needs attention. It wouldn't take you long. Have any interest?"

"Sure." A wave of nervous energy flooded through Lin's body. "You need it done pretty soon?"

Kurt gave a nod. "We'll be finishing up the renovation pretty soon. You have time to squeeze it in over the next couple of weeks?"

"I think so. I could come by and see what you want done, and then we can talk about the timeline."

"Great, thanks." Kurt gave Lin the address. "It's right in town. Come by anytime. I'm working at the house most of the day." The man started away. "It's right next to the Founders Inn and Restaurant."

Lin's heart pounded with apprehension.

***

All day while she worked mowing lawns, pulling weeds, and planting flowers, Lin thought about the upcoming landscaping job at the house in town right near the Founders Inn and Restaurant. It was the same house that Jeff had been doing renovation work on and where he had met Mrs. Perkins and heard her tale of men toiling late at night in the small lot behind the restaurant.

Pulling her truck to the curb in front of island historian, Anton Wilson's antique Cape-style house, Lin hoped he might be at home so she could talk to him about the history of the section of town where Mrs. Perkins's houses were located.

Lin hauled her mower and gardening bag from the truck's bed and she and Nicky walked around the house to the backyard. The dog shot ahead of her hoping to find Anton sitting on the deck.

"Carolin." Anton looked up. He held a book in one hand and was leaning to the side in his chair so that he could reach down and scratch the dog's ears with his other hand. "Is it gardening day?" Anton was absent-minded and could never remember when Lin was scheduled to work in his yard.

Lin smiled. "Yes, it's gardening day." Pushing the mower to the side of the yard and setting down her bag of tools, she stepped up onto the deck and sat down across the table from Anton. The man offered her a cold drink and after some general chit-chit, Lin brought up what was on her mind.

"Why are you wondering about that part of town?" Anton questioned.

Lin told the historian about Mrs. Perkins and what she'd claimed to see going on behind the restaurant the other night. "I've been asked to landscape the front and side yards of the house." She looked pointedly at Anton. "It's a coincidence, isn't it?"

Anton looked over the top of his glasses at Lin. "Interesting." The short, wiry man stood up abruptly and headed for the door to the house. "I'll be right back."

Anton knew everything about the island and, more importantly, he also knew that Lin was able to see ghosts. After several minutes had passed, he returned to the deck carrying several books. "The Founders Inn and Restaurant, you say? I haven't been there for nearly a year. It's a very small place. Lovely décor and atmosphere. Excellent food and service."

Lin smiled and waited as Anton flipped through one of the books.

"Could you bring up a map of that area on your phone?" Anton had his nose stuck in the book. "I need to see it in detail."

Lin tapped at her phone and then placed it on the table in front of the man so he could see the screen.

"Why can't they make these things bigger?" Anton scrunched up his face as he perused the small map showing on Lin's phone.

Lin chuckled. "They do. They're called laptops."

Anton ignored the comment. "This is a very old section of Nantucket town." He moved his head from the book to the phone screen. "The houses and the inn and restaurant in question are located in the historic district. Some of the buildings on these streets date from the mid to late-eighteenth century and are mostly built of wood. After the American Revolution to the mid 1800's, the whaling industry brought wealth to the island so sea captains and town merchants began to build more ornate homes and structures in the Federal and Georgian styles, either in brick or wood." Anton looked at Lin. "I'm not surprised that ghosts appear in that section of town."

"Did anything ever happen there that might cause spirits to be appearing now?"

"I'll have to look into that." Anton gave a nod and then stood up. "Are you done for the day? Do you have any other clients to see after me?"

"I just have your yard left to mow and weed."

"Let's take a walk into town then. Let's have a look at that historic area."

Nicky leapt to his feet with a woof, ready for an adventure.

"But your garden, and the lawn," Lin sputtered.

A Haunted Invitation

"I won't have time to come back until late in the week."

Anton collected the books he had brought out and started for the door of his house to put them inside. "The lawn can wait. We have more important things to attend to."

CHAPTER 3

With his arms pumping as he walked, Anton set a brisk pace for their walk into town. The historian's house was in one of the neighborhoods just at the edge of Nantucket town and it only took them ten minutes to reach the tiny rotary with the monument in the center and then walk down Main Street to the side roads of the historic district. Tourists strolled along the brick and stone sidewalks past the former homes of sea captains and wealthy business owners on their way to stores, restaurants, or down to the docks to see the boats.

Lin kept pace with Anton and Nicky's little legs moved quickly to keep right next to the man as he hurried along the street.

"What do we hope to see?" Lin asked.

"I want to take a close look around. I don't know what we'll discover, but getting a good sense of the area may help us as things move forward."

Lin knew what Anton meant about things moving forward. It wasn't a coincidence that Mrs. Perkins relayed her tale of a disturbed night's sleep to Jeff. Something was brewing and Lin and Anton knew it would involve her eventually.

They turned onto Fairview Street and walked past several large homes before arriving at the corner where the Founders Inn and Restaurant was located. The place didn't open until dinner time so the back lot was empty except for two cars parked close to the building. The lot was small, surrounded on three sides with large trees and a white picket fence, and was tucked discreetly behind the inn.

Anton walked over to the lot, stopped abruptly, and stared.

"What?" Lin tried to follow his gaze.

"So this is where Mrs. Perkins said the hullabaloo went on the other night." Anton had his hands on his hips and was turning his head from side-to-side to take in the scene. He kicked his toe in the stone dust. "The lot isn't paved. It's hard-packed stone dust. Too bad we weren't here on the night Mrs. Perkins saw the activity. We could have checked the lot to see if it looked like things had been dragged around the ground." Anton let his eyes roam about the back of the four-story wooden building, around the lot, and to the periphery of the property. Nicky had his nose to the ground sniffing as he rushed about the space. "Do you sense anything, Carolin?"

Lin took in a deep breath. "I just feel edgy, kind of a low-level anxiety. I don't think it has to do with anything except my own nerves."

Anton and Lin heard someone call her name. Recognizing Jeff's voice, Lin turned and saw her boyfriend diagonally across the street coming down the front steps of a three-story red brick mansion that had dark blue shutters at each of its windows. A black, wrought-iron fence enclosed a small front yard and a brick walkway led to the glossy front door under a portico with two white columns standing sentry on either side.

Lin waved and headed to meet Jeff who was walking over to them. Jeff greeted Lin with a hug and a kiss and then shook hands with Anton. "I didn't expect to see you two down this way."

Lin explained that after hearing Mrs. Perkins's story, Anton thought that they should come down and take a look around just to get a better sense of the area.

"What do you make of it?" Anton asked Jeff for his opinion.

Jeff looked surprised to be asked such a question. "I, well, I don't know." He looked at Lin. "What does Lin say? She's the expert."

Lin gave a nervous chuckle. "I'm not really. I don't know anything. I just follow...." She glanced around to be sure they were alone on the sidewalk and then she lowered her voice. "I just follow the ghosts' leads."

Jeff nodded. "Kurt said he met you at Viv's bookstore this morning. He's pleased that you'll handle the landscaping for the house."

"Is he around? I should take a look since I'm here anyway."

The three crossed the quiet side street and Nicky ran after them. As they approached the house that was being renovated, a short, sturdy, woman with nicely-styled white-blonde hair headed towards them from down the street. "Oh, Jeff. Hello. How are things going today?" The woman looked to be in her early seventies.

Jeff introduced his companions to Mrs. Perkins, the owner of the mansion. "This is Lin Coffin. Kurt's hired her to landscape the front of the house and the small side yard."

Mrs. Perkins shook hands with Lin. "You work with Leonard Reed? I hear very good things about your work."

Jeff gave the woman a run-down of the day's progress. In the middle of his description, Mrs. Perkins let out a yawn and, embarrassed, she clasped her hand over her mouth. "I'm so sorry. I didn't sleep well again last night." The woman glanced across the street to the rear lot of the inn-restaurant.

Jeff took a quick look at Lin who made eye contact with him and gave a slight nod.

"Were the men working again last night?" Jeff asked.

"Oh, my, what a racket." Mrs. Perkins shook her head. "I can't imagine what they're doing over there so late at night or why what they're doing has to be done after midnight. I need to get to the bottom of this. I didn't move to town to be awake all night."

Lin took the opportunity to ask some questions even though she knew some of the answers already. "Where are the men working?"

Mrs. Perkins waved her hand towards the lot behind the inn and restaurant building. "Over there. It goes on all night long." She reached up and ran her fingers over her pearl necklace. "I also own that house opposite. I'm staying there while my home is being renovated. I can see the men right from the upstairs bedroom windows."

"How long has the late-night work been going on?" Lin asked.

"It started one night last week. This week, it's happened the past two nights in a row."

"Could you talk to the inn-restaurant owner about it?" Lin flicked her eyes to Jeff and Anton wondering what the owner would say if Mrs. Perkins inquired about the nighttime noise.

"In fact, I did speak to him." Mrs. Perkins scowled. "I marched over there a few hours ago. I've eaten at that restaurant many times, the food is quite good. It's a small dining room so it can be hard to get reservations, but it's well worth the trouble. I'm acquainted with the owner from frequenting the place." The woman's cheeks flushed. "I asked about the workmen and the noise.

A Haunted Invitation

Guess what the owner said?" Mrs. Perkins didn't wait to hear any guesses. "He didn't know what I was talking about. Well, we'll see about that, won't we?"

A cool shiver ran over Lin's skin. She took a quick look over to the lot. "Could it be possible that those men are using the lot once the restaurant closes?"

Mrs. Perkins's lips pursed into a pout and she blinked at Lin. "Do you mean without the owner's knowledge? For their own purposes?" She made a grunting noise. "I didn't think of that. How could they do that without the owner knowing?" Turning her head from Jeff to Anton to Lin, the woman squinted her eyes and glared in the direction of the lot. "Perhaps the police should be called again." Mrs. Perkins addressed her comments to Lin. "I called the police the other night, but before the officers arrived, those men hid in a little gulley over there at the edge of the lot near the fence. Isn't that suspicious?"

"What did the police do?" Lin questioned.

"Barely a thing. They got out of the cruiser, flashed a light around, and got back in and drove away. Not exactly what I expected. I thought there would be more investigation than that." Mrs. Perkins tugged at the cuff of her navy blue jacket.

Anton piped up. "What goes on over there? How many men are working so late?"

The woman tapped her finger against her chin.

"How many? Maybe fifteen? I didn't count them. They take big containers from near the back door of the restaurant. The boxes seem quite heavy. The men push them and try to drag them across the lot to a truck."

"Why don't they just drive closer instead of dragging the containers?" Anton shifted his position on the sidewalk to get a better view of the lot.

"You'll have to ask them, I'm afraid." Mrs. Perkins frowned.

"Do you hear them talking?" Lin cocked her head.

"I hear them jabbering and laughing. I don't understand a word they're saying though."

Lin got an idea. "Are they speaking a foreign language?"

"I don't think so. I'm just not close enough to hear the words clearly." Mrs. Perkins narrowed her eyes. "Last night, I wondered if they were drunk. There was so much laughter and back-slapping and what-not. Whatever they're doing, they better finish up quick or I'll have to make a stink to the town authorities." Shaking her head in disgust, she sighed and shifted her attention to Jeff. "Well, enough about the nighttime nuisance. Why don't we go inside so that I can see today's progress?" Mrs. Perkins said goodbye to Lin and Anton and she and Jeff headed for the front door of the mansion.

A Haunted Invitation

Jeff nodded to Anton and gave Lin a warm smile. "I'll see you later."

Once Mrs. Perkins and Jeff had disappeared into the house, Anton turned to Lin. "I think a late night visit to the area is in order."

A flush of nervousness passed through Lin's body. "I don't know. I don't want to push my nose into something. I haven't seen a ghost. I haven't been asked for help."

Nicky woofed and wagged his little stub of a tail.

"If we come back tonight, Carolin, you might just see a ghost." Anton started down the sidewalk. "Perhaps they don't know where to find you."

Running her finger nervously over her horseshoe necklace as she watched the historian walk away, Lin groaned and muttered, "They always know where to find me."

CHAPTER 4

"Is Mrs. Perkins the only one who can see those men working back there?" Viv set a platter of appetizers on the deck table and took a seat across from her cousin. Nicky and Queenie sat under the table in the hopes that one of the young women might share some of the food. Viv must have gotten the message because she slipped the cat and dog two small pieces of chicken satay.

"I don't know. We don't even know for sure that they're ghosts. They could just be men. Live men." Lin scooped some hummus and toasted rounds onto her plate.

Viv lifted her glass of iced tea. "So if we go down there tonight, will we see them?"

"I don't know. I don't know what's going on."

Viv dipped a piece of the chicken into some peanut sauce. "I bet they're ghosts. Plenty of normal people run into ghosts on-island. There are a number of books recounting people's experiences seeing ghosts on Nantucket. Anton even wrote a book on the subject."

A Haunted Invitation

"What do you mean 'normal' people?" Lin narrowed her eyes.

"You know what I mean. *Regular* people, not people with special gifts. Sometimes ghosts show themselves to regular people, not just people like you." Viv sipped from her glass. "I'd actually like to see a ghost."

Lin looked at her cousin in astonishment. "You? Really?"

"I'm getting used to your adventures." Viv looked out at the shadows gathering over her back lawn. "Although, if I did see a ghost, I would probably freak out."

Lin chuckled. "We won't know for sure what your reaction will be until it happens."

Viv's expression turned serious. "If Mrs. Perkins can see the ghosts, then you'll probably be able to see them, too."

Lin gave a shrug. "I really don't know how it all works. I don't know why people can sometimes see ghosts. I don't even know why I can see them."

"What do you think is going on behind that restaurant?" Viv bit into a piece of her chicken appetizer. "What do you think those men are doing? Why are they showing themselves now? Out of the blue? Nothing's changed down there in that part of town. All of a sudden, ghosts are spending the night working down there behind the restaurant?"

"From what Mrs. Perkins says, the men sound

happy as they work." Lin smiled and joked. "I sure wouldn't be happy working from midnight to dawn."

"Did Anton say anything about what he thought might be going on?" Viv put a few more appetizers on her plate. "Does he know the history of that part of town?"

"Anton knows a lot about the buildings and the different waves of activity that happened on the island, like the settling of the island, the whaling industry, the decline of the economy that led to a drop in population, but he doesn't know anything specifically about the building where the ghosts are working." Lin poured more iced tea into her glass from the pitcher. "But you know Anton. He's going to research the place to try and come up with an idea."

"That could be helpful." Viv nodded and then made eye contact with her cousin. "Have you decided to go down there tonight?"

The corners of Lin's mouth turned down. "I'm not sure I should."

"Why the hesitation? You always jump right in when a ghost shows up."

Lin looked at Viv and tried to explain her feelings. "It's like … I feel like I haven't been asked. The ghosts usually want me to help with something. I haven't had a visit from a spirit, so I think it's none of my business."

"But, what about the timing of all this? Jeff

A Haunted Invitation

hears about these ghosts right before you tell him about your skill. Maybe it all worked out that way because some ghost wants you to know about those men working at night."

Lin raised an eyebrow. "Why do you always make sense?"

"It happens to be *my* special skill." Viv chuckled. "So, are we going for a midnight stroll tonight?"

Lin dipped a toasted bread round into the hummus. "Maybe."

Nicky wagged his little tail and woofed.

Viv smiled at the small creature. "That dog is always ready for adventure."

***

Under the glimmering streetlamps, the cousins ambled down the cobblestone roads of town heading for the historic neighborhood that Lin had visited earlier in the day. Nicky and Queenie, much to their dismay, were left locked in the house. Lin had texted Anton about the plans to make the late-night visit and he replied saying he would meet them on the corner of Fairview and Main Streets. A cool breeze came off the ocean and Viv zipped up her sweater.

Viv had insisted on taking a flashlight on the midnight adventure even though Lin said it wouldn't be needed. If ghosts were present, they shouldn't be shining a flashlight on them she'd told her cousin. When Viv said that having the heavy item in her hand made her feel safer because she could use it as a weapon, Lin chuckled picturing Viv swinging the metal object at an insubstantial ghost.

Approaching the corner of Main and Fairview, Viv slipped her hand through her cousin's arm and pulled her closer.

"I thought you were eager to see spirits." Lin raised an eyebrow.

"I think I left my courage back at the house."

"They're just ghosts. Nothing will happen. It will be okay." Lin tried to reassure her trembling cousin.

"What if they're real men doing something illegal and we walk up and they see us? They might try to attack us."

"Then I guess it's a good thing you brought your weapon," Lin joked.

The night was overcast and there were fewer streetlamps on Fairview Street, so the cousins turned onto the darker road with some feelings of apprehension. A figure stepped from the shadows causing both girls to jump. Lin gasped in surprise and Viv almost screamed before realizing it was Anton who stood before them.

"Ugh. Don't do that to us." Viv wrapped her arms around her body and sucked in a few deep breaths.

"Hello to you, too." Anton was dressed in black

slacks, black shoes, and a black shirt and sweater.

"I see you have your snooping outfit on." Lin smiled at the ever-prepared historian.

"One can never be too careful." Anton adjusted his black-rimmed glasses.

"Have you heard anything coming from the lot?" Lin looked down the street to see if she could see anything.

"Nothing. It's been quiet so far."

"How should we go about this?" Lin questioned. "Should we just walk down the street like everything's normal?"

Anton nodded. "I think that's best. Let's walk slowly. If we hear or see anything, we can step into someone's yard so we aren't visible to whoever is in the back lot."

"Let's not speak to each other either." Viv stepped closer to Lin. "We don't want anyone to hear us coming."

The three quietly headed down the dark sidewalk to the inn-restaurant building moving together closely, side by side. Here and there, a light could be seen shining in one of the windows of the houses they passed.

When they were only one building away, Anton held up his index finger to indicate that they should halt. "I don't hear anything," he whispered. "Let's creep up to the lot in case the men suddenly appear."

Moving a few inches at a time, the three

advanced. In addition to the white picket fence, a tall thick hedge separated the lot from the house next to it, so the group of sleuths slipped behind and crouched down to peek through the greenery.

"Nothing," Lin whispered, gazing at the lot.

Viv swiveled her head around looking in all directions. "Could they just show up at any time, like, just suddenly appear in the empty lot without any warning?"

Lin shrugged, and suspecting that it might be a long evening, she slid down to the ground and sat. Viv did the same, but Anton preferred to stand so that he wouldn't get dirt or grass on his slacks.

"Can you see any marks in the gravel?" Lin pushed some branches to the side so she could stare through the hedge. "Does it look like any activity already went on here tonight?"

"None that I can see." Anton scanned the area.

Two security spotlights attached to the back of the restaurant shined into the empty space where Mrs. Perkins claimed to have seen the men working. Lin wondered if the woman might have dreamt the entire thing. She thought of asking Viv's boyfriend, John, who had a friend at the police station if Mrs. Perkins did indeed make a call to the police reporting the disturbance the other night. The woman might have dreamt that, too.

The cool, damp night air chilled Lin as she sat on the ground with the thought that this might be nothing but a wild goose chase swirling around in her head.

A long hour passed with the three of them sitting, or in Anton's case, standing, waiting for something to happen. Lin's eyelids grew heavy and they made several attempts to slam shut. Every time she nearly dozed off, her head would loll to the side and then she'd snap upright.

As Lin took in a deep breath and shifted around on the grass trying to keep alert, Viv, sitting close to her, suddenly snorted and then jolted. Blinking her eyes, Viv looked around disoriented. "I fell asleep," she whispered.

Viv's sudden snort made her cousin giggle. The oddness of sitting behind a hedge waiting for ghosts to show up struck Lin as absurd, and that, in combination with Viv's oinking sound and flailing jolt from slumber, caused Lin to chuckle and then she couldn't stop.

Anton's attempt to hush her only made Lin laugh harder.

Viv gave her cousin a playful push. "Stop it."

Lin's mirth became contagious and in a few seconds, Viv was howling along with her cousin.

"Hush, you two. For heaven's sake." Anton glanced around to see if any lights were coming on inside the nearby houses. "Get up, get up." He tugged on the young women's sweaters. "Good grief. Someone will call the police on us."

In between a few more guffaws, Lin managed to roll to her side and push herself up to standing position. "Sorry," she gasped as she reached for Viv's arm and tugged her to her feet.

Viv wiped tears from her cheeks and then moved her hands to her belly. "My stomach hurts from laughing."

"Let's get out of here." Anton put a hand on each girl's elbow and pushed them away from the lot to head back to Main Street. "Remind me never to join you in a surveillance task ever again."

Viv released one more hoot of laughter as she stumbled along.

"Laugh, yes," Anton blustered. "I am an upstanding member of this community. Imagine me getting arrested for disturbing the peace along with the two female hyenas in my company."

Once they reached Main Street, Viv and Lin were finally able to collect themselves. Standing under a streetlamp, Anton continued to scold them. "That was a waste." Despite his initial annoyance at the two fools grinning in front of him, the man could not help but smile. "Good Lord, you two are terrible influences, and even worse detectives."

"Nothing happened. We watched for over an hour." Lin tried to defend their sudden burst of levity. She then shared her idea that Mrs. Perkins might have dreamt the entire nocturnal episode that she thought she saw from her window.

"It might be a good idea to ask John's friend at the police station if a disturbance call about the noise came in last week," Viv said, but then thought of something else. "Although, Mrs. Perkins could have dreamt the whole thing, woke up thinking it was real, and called the police anyway. So I suppose finding out whether she called or not might not be that revealing."

"Jeff told me that Mrs. Perkins has a friend who lives a few doors down from her on Fairview Street. If we could talk to the friend, we could find out if she heard or saw the men in the lot. If both of the women saw the workmen, then it had to have happened and wasn't just the woman's dream."

"Good idea." Anton nodded. "Perhaps when you're working on the landscaping for the house, you'll run into the friend and you can speak with her about the alleged noise."

When Anton said the word 'alleged,' a zing of anxiety zapped across Lin's forehead.

The man yawned and turned to head up Main Street. "Now let's put an end to our evening misadventure."

Viv started after him. "I'll second that statement."

Lin was about to follow when a frigid blast of air engulfed her and kept her from moving forward. Swallowing hard, she turned slowly to look back down Fairview Street.

A man stood in the middle of the road, staring after Lin. Dressed in the clothes of the early 1900's, he removed his cap and gave the slightest of nods before his whole body began to glimmer brighter and brighter until his form seemed to burn out like a Fourth of July sparkler on a stick.

Lin blinked. The man was gone.

Viv called to her cousin and Lin turned around. When Viv saw the look on Lin's face, she asked, "What's wrong with you? You look like you've seen a...."

It only took a half-second for Viv to realize what was wrong and a look of alarm to spread over her face. "Oh. You *did* see a ghost."

CHAPTER 5

Lin pulled weeds out of the garden patch at the front of the house that was being renovated on Fairview Street. Nicky sniffed around the small space and then plopped down in the corner to watch his owner work. Lin had been awake for a good part of the night, tossing and turning and thinking about the new ghost who had appeared in the middle of the street as she and Viv and Anton walked away from the restaurant's back lot. She reported what she'd seen to her companions and on their late-night walk back to their houses, they proposed reasons for the ghost's sudden materialization and discussed why the workmen didn't show up in the lot. No good reasons emerged from the conversation and they concluded that more research and investigation would be needed.

Lin thought about the ghost. When he made eye contact with her, ideas and sensations swirled around in her head so quickly that it almost made her dizzy. She knew that it would take time to sort out what the ghost wanted, or needed, from her.

The man's style of clothing suggested the early-nineteen hundreds so Anton was going to look into what was going on in town during that timeframe.

Deep in thought as she weeded the patch of garden, Lin startled when a woman spoke to her.

The woman stood on the sidewalk just outside the fence that enclosed the front garden. She had silver-white hair, cut short, with long bangs hanging over her forehead. Slender, well-dressed and stylish, she looked at Lin with a friendly smile. "Hello. I'm looking for my friend. Have you seen her wandering around down this way?"

Lin stood up and dusted off her soil-covered hands. "Do you mean Mrs. Perkins? I haven't seen anyone go in or out since I've been here."

The woman rolled her eyes. "She was supposed to meet me. Where has she gotten off to?"

"If I see her," Lin said, "I'll tell her you're looking for her."

"I'm Linda McQueen, Mrs. Perkins's good friend." She extended her hand to shake with Lin.

Instead of accepting the hand-shake, Lin gestured a wave "hello" with her hand. "It's best not to shake with me. I'm a dirty mess."

"Oh, a bit of dirt doesn't worry me." Mrs. McQueen looked up at the front door of the mansion. "The work is coming along nicely. Have you been inside? Have you seen it?"

Lin shook her head. "I'm just doing the landscaping." Hoping to get the woman talking, she asked, "You live down the street from here?"

"I do. We've lived there for ages. Before we owned, we came to the island every summer. We decided that owning instead of renting was the smarter thing to do." Linda pointed to the house near the lot. "Polly is staying over there in the other place she owns until this house is finished."

Lin blinked for a second wondering who Polly was and then realized it was Mrs. Perkins. "Mrs. Perkins told me about the recent late-night noise that has been going on in the neighborhood."

Taking a look over her shoulder to the lot, Mrs. McQueen shook her head and her face clouded. "What on earth could those men be working on so late at night? Polly went to talk to the inn owner about the noise. He said he didn't know what she was talking about." The woman put a hand on her hip. "Really? Polly heard and saw those men working in the lot on at least three different occasions. How could the owner not know what was happening back there? I think he was just blowing Polly off. Of course, he must know what's going on."

"Were the men there last night?" Lin wondered if the group showed up after she and Viv and Anton had left.

"Thankfully, no. Polly said it was a night of blessed silence."

"Have you heard the disturbance in the lot?" Lin asked.

Linda brushed at her bangs. "No, I haven't. My husband hasn't either. We're both very sound sleepers. Although, last night, I did wake up to the sound of laughter. We like to sleep with the windows open. It must have been someone passing by or someone having a late-night gathering, but it was very loud."

Lin's cheeks turned pink when she realized that Mrs. McQueen had heard her and Viv's outburst of laughter late last night. Thankfully, the woman had not peered out of her window to see Lin and Viv stumbling up the street roaring with laughter as Anton berated them.

Returning the topic of conversation back to the men, Lin asked, "Did Mrs. Perkins tell you what those men in the lot were doing? Could she see what they were up to?"

"They were moving big containers. Polly said they looked very heavy."

"Did she say if the men went into the restaurant to get the containers?"

Mrs. McQueen's forehead creased in thought and she glanced over to the lot. "You know, I don't recall. That first night, Polly said she watched them for hours, but I just can't remember if she said the men went inside the building." She shook her head. "I wonder where Polly is."

The sound of a door opening caused Lin and Mrs. McQueen to turn towards the front of the house. Mrs. Perkins, dressed in a blue skirt and starched white blouse, came down the steps.

At the sight of her friend, relief spread over Mrs. McQueen's face. "There you are, Polly. I wondered where you'd gotten off to."

Mrs. Perkins walked over to her friend and put her hand on her arm. "You look flustered. Is something wrong?"

"Oh, no. Lin and I were just discussing those late-night workers and their noise." Mrs. McQueen patted her friend's hand. "How are the renovations coming?"

"Everything looks lovely." Mrs. Perkins nodded at Lin.

"You had a quiet night here?" Lin asked Mrs. Perkins. "No workers last night?"

"None, thank heavens. I slept very soundly."

"I was wondering if you noticed how the men were dressed when you saw them in the lot?" Lin didn't want the women to leave just yet.

Mrs. Perkins looked at Lin with a puzzled expression. "Dressed?"

"What were they wearing?"

One of the woman's eyebrows lifted. "Hmmm. Let me think."

After a few seconds passed, Lin asked, "Uniforms? Jeans? Did they look like they belonged to a company or maybe were just working on their own?"

"No jeans." Mrs. Perkins shook her head. "They all had on trousers, most had on white shirts with the sleeves rolled up. A couple had on a jumpsuit, made of cloth, like workers used to wear over their clothes, you know, with a zipper up the front." She mimed zipping the front of a jumpsuit. "Some had on caps, like a jockey wears, only sort of made of a tweed material." She nodded. "Oh, and a few had on buttoned-up vests."

"Vests?" Lin asked. "Like winter vests?"

"No. Vests made of matching material to the trousers."

"Seems sort of dressed up to be moving heavy boxes, doesn't it?" Lin noted.

"It does, now that you mention it. I didn't think of it at the time."

"You said you called the police about it."

"I did on the first night." Mrs. Perkins made a face. "I wasn't very impressed with them. They got out of their patrol car, glanced around the back of the restaurant for a second, and left. That was it."

"Where did you say the workers were when the police arrived?"

Frowning, Mrs. Perkins said, "They hid in a little gulley or ditch on the edge of the lot."

"That seems pretty odd." Lin looked over to the lot wondering if Mrs. Perkins had dreamt the whole thing. "How did they hide the things they were moving? Weren't the boxes right out in the open when the police arrived?"

Reaching up to rub her temple, Mrs. Perkins stared blankly at Lin. "I really don't recall."

A Haunted Invitation

"Why don't we go inside and you can show me the latest work that's been done," Mrs. McQueen suggested.

The two women said goodbye to Lin and went inside the brick mansion to view the renovation work.

Lin watched them go and then looked down at Nicky sitting near the fence. "Strange doings, huh, Nick?"

The dog let out a woof.

"I think we need to talk this over with Viv." Lin winked at the small brown creature and smiled. "And with Queenie, too."

Lin spent another hour working on the front garden, pulling out weeds, inspecting the perennials that were there, and making some notes about what new plants should be put in. Busy with her sketchbook, she didn't hear Jeff come up behind her. As he wrapped her in a bear hug, she let out a yip of surprise and Nicky woke up from his nap on the grass to greet Jeff with a happy jig around the man's legs.

Bending to scratch the dog's ears, Jeff looked around the garden. "You're making progress."

Lin smiled brightly at the good-looking carpenter. "A very small bit of progress."

Jeff put his arm around Lin's waist.

Lin pointed at the old garden beds. "I have to assess what's here and what should be done to enhance the look of the property. Leonard is coming by tomorrow to give his opinion. We were thinking of adding some heirloom plants to the landscape."

"I'm sure it will look great." Jeff looked up to the front door of the house. "Is Mrs. Perkins inside?"

Lin nodded. "She went in with a friend of hers about an hour or so ago."

Jeff lowered his voice. "Mrs. Perkins had a meeting scheduled with the project manager. There's a big glitch. The electrical wiring isn't up to code and when they were making the necessary changes, they found a major plumbing issue that's going to add a ton of money to the original estimate. Mrs. Perkins will not be pleased."

"What if she doesn't want to pay? Is there a workaround that can be done?"

"She has to do it. The place is old and isn't up to code." Jeff frowned. "I decided to go to another job this morning to avoid being here when they broke the news to her."

Lin narrowed her eyes and smiled. "Coward."

Jeff grinned. "In some cases, you bet I am."

"What will be involved?" Lin asked.

"Tearing out some of the walls, putting in new pipes. The work that needs to be done is going to add to the timeline, that's for sure." Jeff shook his head. "I'm sure glad I'm not the project manager."

"From the few times I've seen Mrs. Perkins, it seems that she's very eager to have the work done so she can move back in." Lin glanced towards the front door. "I'm done here for the day." She raised an eyebrow at Jeff. "Maybe it's a good time to leave."

"I'll walk you to your truck." Jeff helped Lin pack up her tools and carry them to her vehicle which was parked two blocks away towards Main Street. "Are we still on for dinner tonight?"

"You bet." Lin slung her canvas bag over her shoulder and the two headed down the sidewalk with the dog trotting behind them. Lin spoke quietly as she told her boyfriend about the previous night's appearance of the new ghost.

"He just stared at you? He didn't speak?"

Lin rolled her eyes. "They never speak. I wish they did. It would make things so much easier."

"How do you know how to help them then?"

Letting out a sigh, Lin shrugged a shoulder. "It can be hard. I'm learning to pay attention to when and where they appear. It's often a clue. Sometimes it's very easy to overlook the important subtlety of the appearance. I need to get better at it."

"Are you afraid of this ghost?" Jeff took hold of Lin's hand protectively.

"No, I'm never really afraid. I'm uncomfortable, at times, anxious that I'm taking too long to figure things out, but not really afraid. I never feel like I'm in harm's way or in danger from a ghost." She let out a nervous chuckle. "Not so far, anyway."

"I'm glad you told me about your, ah ... skill."

Jeff glanced sideways at the brunette walking beside him. "It means a lot to me."

"I hope you don't change your mind about that." Lin smiled up at Jeff and he leaned down and gave her a sweet kiss. Nicky ran a few yards ahead of the couple wagging his little tail.

Lin squeezed Jeff's hand. "I'm thinking of enlisting you as an assistant ghost investigator."

As they loaded the tools into the bed of the truck, Jeff winked. "At your service, Ma'am." He glanced back down the street in the direction of Mrs. Perkins's house and added, "Just remember what a coward I am when things go wrong."

CHAPTER 6

Lin worked the edging tool around the new flower bed she was creating at the side of the client's patio and she jumped when Nicky let out a joyful bark. The dog darted to the side of the house to greet Leonard, Lin's landscaping partner, and when the man bent to give the little dog a pat, the creature started a game of tag by rushing away and then charging back at Leonard. As Leonard's hearty laugh filled the air, Lin leaned on her tool and stopped to watch the crazy game.

"What's got into him?" Leonard pretended to grab the animal as he zoomed past.

"He's happy to see you." Lin chuckled. "There's no humidity today so he has lots of energy."

"He's about to drain all of my energy." Leonard was tall, and as a result of years of landscaping work, his shoulders were broad and his arms were strong and muscular. He had a full head of dark hair and despite being in his early sixties, just a few strands of gray showed at his temples.

Nicky stopped his play and pressed against

Leonard's leg while the big man scratched the dog's back causing one of the canine's rear legs to lift and pump in reaction to the pleasant itching.

Lin had placed a picnic basket on a blanket under a shade tree. She and Leonard had planned to meet for lunch to finish the landscaping design of the new client's back lawn and pool area. The two plopped down on the blanket and Lin removed the containers of rice, grilled chicken with mushrooms and onions, and slices of bruschetta from the basket and placed them on the blanket. The dog received a small bowl of plain chicken and he sat at the side of the blanket eagerly chewing the tasty lunch.

While they ate, Lin and Leonard discussed their ideas for the planting design around the pool and talked about some of the new clients who had recently contacted them and which ones they should take on.

"We should think about permanently hiring some help." Leonard wiped at his mouth with a napkin. "We're getting more client inquiries than we can handle on our own."

They weighed the pros and cons of hiring the middle-aged couple who often helped them out on big jobs and then Lin told Leonard about starting on Mrs. Perkins's front yard. After discussion about the perennials that should be included in both the front and side gardens, Lin brought up the story of the men working late in the small lot behind the inn-restaurant near Mrs. Perkins's house.

"What's that about?" Leonard lifted a forkful of rice from his container. "Why would they need to be working all night? Has Mrs. Perkins asked the restaurant owner what's going on over there?"

Lin nodded and took a sip of her seltzer. "The owner said he doesn't know what she's talking about."

Leonard's eyes widened. "How does he not know?"

Shrugging a shoulder Lin said, "Maybe he's doing something illegal?"

"Huh." Leonard let out a grunt. After thinking for a minute, he came up with an idea. "Did the woman dream the whole thing?"

"I don't know. It's possible. I wondered the same thing."

"Is this woman just looking for attention? Or did she have too much to drink those nights and just think she saw those men out there?"

A look of surprise crossed over Lin's face. "I didn't think of that." Lin had kept her ability to see ghosts a secret from her business partner, but she often wished that he knew about her skill so that she could freely discuss things with him. "I'm inclined to believe what she's saying though."

"Why?"

One side of Lin's mouth formed a frown. "The woman really seems to believe it. She couldn't get drunk every night and talk herself into seeing those men."

"Couldn't she?" Leonard leaned back against the trunk of the tree and the dog contentedly snuggled next to him. "You know how people can get themselves into a tizzy, an idea goes wild and convinces the person into making a big deal out of it."

Lin's forehead scrunched up as she considered Leonard's statement. Did what Mrs. Perkins say about the late-night workers have nothing to do with the ghost she saw on Fairview Street the other night? Lin couldn't explain why, but she was pretty sure the occurrences were connected. "I don't think that's the case here."

"What do you think it is then?" Leonard took a swig from his water bottle.

"I don't know. I wanted to hear what you think."

Adjusting his back against the tree, Leonard closed his eyes. "I told you what I think."

"Well, suppose for a moment that your idea is wrong." Lin smiled. "I realize that you being wrong is probably impossible, but what would your second explanation be?"

Leonard opened one eye. "Ghosts?"

Lin almost dropped her can of seltzer and had to grab at it with both hands to keep it from hitting the blanket. With wide eyes, she stared at the man sitting across from her.

Leonard grinned and pushed himself forward to reach for his water bottle. "I'm kidding, Coffin.

A Haunted Invitation

Maybe it's something illegal, like you said."

Lin let out a soft sigh of relief that Leonard was joking about ghosts. "Like what though? The men are moving big containers."

Leonard shook his head. "Drugs? Booze?"

A little shiver of apprehension buzzed down Lin's back when she heard the word booze. "Alcohol? It isn't Prohibition. What could anyone do that was illegal involving alcohol?"

"Just throwing ideas out there." Leonard scratched the dog's ears. "How about money laundering?"

"Wouldn't money laundering be done online?"

Leonard looked across the green lawn to the thicket of trees lining the rear of the property and watched some butterflies moving among the wildflowers. "What about moving valuables? Like antiques or paintings, statues, antiquities?"

Lin sat up. "Huh. That's a good idea." She pondered Leonard's suggestion wondering if the ghost-men had actually used the building long-ago to store valuable stolen art objects and then shipped them out when it was safe. "Interesting." Lin thought about the other question that plagued her ... why are the ghosts showing up now? What's happened that has the ghost-men showing up now? And what does the ghost who appeared in the street want from her?

Leonard snapped his fingers. "Come back to Earth, Coffin."

Lin blinked. "I was just thinking about what you said. It's a definite possibility."

"The other possibility is that the woman was in a drunken state and worked herself into a fever-pitch over what she thinks she saw and heard. It's probably just some confusion." Leonard stretched. "How could a bunch of guys work all night behind that restaurant and this person is the only one who is concerned about it? Wouldn't other people in that neighborhood be angry about the ruckus the workers are supposedly making?"

Lin frowned. "Stop being so logical." She gave the man a playful bop on his leg, but then thought to ask, "Do you know any history of that neighborhood?"

"Not much." Leonard ran his hand through his hair. "Fairview Street and Tangerine Street are some of the oldest in Nantucket town. When the economy started to boom on the island from whaling, those two streets became the place to be for the newly wealthy. Larger, fancier houses were built for the prosperous merchants and the sea captains and the ship owners." Leonard eyed Lin. "You know, Coffin, there are supposed to be a lot of ghosts down that way."

Lin chuckled trying not to seem flustered by the man's talk of ghosts. "The whole island is supposed to have a lot of ghosts on it." She looked directly at her landscaping partner. "Is that what you think is going on behind the restaurant? A bunch of ghosts are moving objects around?"

"You never know." Leonard reached for his backpack, removed a lunchbox sized cooler bag, unzipped it, and took out a plastic container. Popping the top off, he rested the container on the blanket between them. "Since you made the lunch today, I made brownies for dessert. There's some caramel swirl in the middle of them."

Lin's eyes went wide as she lifted one of the brownies from the box and took a bite. "Ohhh." She moaned at the combined deliciousness of the chocolate and caramel flavors. "I think I've gone to Heaven."

Leonard took a bite of a brownie and rolled his eyes at Lin's comment. "It's just a brownie."

"Oh, no, it isn't." Lin was shaking her head. "This is so much more than a brownie." Reaching into the box for a second one, Lin said, "I told you this before, but I think you've made a career mistake. You should open a bakery."

Leonard pushed himself up off the blanket. "And I've told you before, I like being outside." He scooped his things off the blanket and gave the dog another scratch behind the ears.

"Maybe you could open a food cart. You know, drive around the island selling your bakery goods." Lin folded the blanket.

Leonard scowled. "Are you trying to get rid of me?"

Lin laughed. "No, but maybe we could expand

from landscaping into baked goods."

The big man ignored his partner's jabbering. "I'm heading over to the Millard's place. They're having a wedding there next weekend. They want more flowers planted."

"Tonight, I'll finish up the design sketches for the garden we're putting in around the pool." Lin pointed to the grassy portion of the yard to the left of the in-ground swimming pool.

"I'll see you tomorrow." Leonard started for the front of the house with Nicky walking him to his truck when the man stopped suddenly and turned back to Lin with an expression of concern on his face. He hesitated for a moment.

"What?" Lin asked.

"I don't know." Leonard shrugged. "Never mind."

"What is it?" Lin insisted.

Leonard gave another shrug, but then he blurted out, "It's nothing. I don't know, I.... Just be careful down on Fairview Street."

As her partner wheeled and walked quickly around the corner of the house, a cold chill traveled down Lin's spine.

CHAPTER 7

"And then he told me to be careful on Fairview Street." Lin walked beside Viv, the two wheeling their bicycles down Viv's driveway to the shed. The cousins had ridden a ten-mile loop on the island bike paths before returning home to make dinner.

Her hands on the handlebars of the bike, Viv used her arm to wipe some sweat from her forehead. There was a quiver in her voice when she commented on Lin's statement. "He did? But, why? Why did Leonard warn you to be careful?"

"I don't know. I don't think Leonard even knows why he said it." Lin leaned her bike against the side of the wood shed. Leonard had some unexplainable sixth sense that alerted him whenever Lin was in danger and several times his premonition had kept her from harm.

"Oh, gosh." Viv kicked off her bike shoes and leaned down to pick them up. "Do you think that ghost you saw down on Fairview Street the other night is dangerous?"

Lin removed her water bottle from the metal

holder on the bicycle frame. "I feel uneasy when I think about being down there on the street, but I can't tell whether it's the ghost or something else that's the reason for the feeling."

Viv threaded her arm through her cousin's and led her to the deck off the rear of her Cape-style house. "You need to be careful. Don't go there alone. Ever. Bring one of us with you. It doesn't matter if it's day or night."

Lin groaned. "Nothing will happen to me."

"Humor me." Viv opened the back door and Lin followed her to the kitchen. Nicky ran to greet the cousins as they entered the house, and Queenie, stretching her back as she woke from a nap, padded over and rubbed against the girls' legs.

"You wouldn't be afraid to go down there with me?" Lin raised an eyebrow at Viv as she patted the dog and cat.

"Well, I might be cautious about it." Viv opened the refrigerator door. "You could take Jeff with you, or maybe, Anton. You can call on me last."

"Thanks." Lin chuckled. "I was thinking of going back down there tonight."

Holding a long loaf of French bread, Viv turned around and gave Lin the eye. "Really? Why?"

"To figure things out." Lin removed a container of soup from the fridge. "The ghost-men didn't show themselves when we were there last. Why didn't they? Why allow Mrs. Perkins to see them, but not me?"

A Haunted Invitation

"Do you think you aren't supposed to see them? I mean, I *never* see them, but I thought maybe I might because Mrs. Perkins could see them." Viv's eyes widened. "Oh. Does Mrs. Perkins have the same ability to see ghosts that you do? If she does, then why do they show themselves to her, but not to you?" Viv cocked her head. "Nobody else in that neighborhood seems to be bothered by the noise the workers make late at night." She placed the bread loaf on the cutting board and started to slice it. "Is that because the ghosts don't show themselves to any other people on that street?"

Lin removed lettuce, tomatoes, cucumbers, and carrots from the refrigerator's vegetable bin. "Those are interesting observations. What could be the reason they would hide from everyone but Mrs. Perkins? Why would only Mrs. Perkins be able to see them?"

Viv sprinkled olive oil into a frying pan and placed the slices of bread into the pan to brown them. "It has to be a clue. Is the ghost you saw the other night part of the group of those workmen or is he a lone spirit?"

"I get the feeling that he's not part of the group, but is related somehow. I feel like he's separate from them, but that those ghost-men have something to do with his appearance."

"Okay, so if he isn't part of the group, then the theory that the workmen are only seen by Mrs. Perkins holds true." Viv used tongs to turn the bread slices. "It's not very clear is it? These ghosts need to speak up, not just stand there staring at you. It's so annoying."

Lin chuckled as she stood next to the stove using a wooden spoon to stir corn chowder in a pot. "It's not how ghosts operate. At least, not my ghosts."

Viv spun around. "*Your* ghosts. Those ghost-workmen may not operate the same way as *your* ghosts. Your ghosts have never tried to hurt you. Your ghosts want help with something. What do these workmen want?"

Lin realized that she had been assuming that all ghosts behaved in the same way. Her cousin's observations sent a flicker of nervousness through her body. Maybe all ghosts weren't benevolent. Maybe all ghosts didn't just want someone's help. The thought chilled Lin.

Viv used the tongs like a baton to emphasize her words by poking the air with them. "That's a reason you need to be careful with these new ghosts. Who knows what they want? Who knows what they're up to? Who knows what they might do?"

Lin swallowed hard. "You're right. We need to figure out what's going on."

Viv straightened up. "You agree with me?"

"Yes. The pattern is different this time. I don't see the ghosts that Mrs. Perkins can see."

"Claims to see." Viv removed the slices of French bread and added mushrooms, chopped

A Haunted Invitation

tomatoes, and olive oil to the pan. "Maybe she's making it up. Maybe she's hallucinating... or she might be drunk and *thinks* she sees men working."

Lin used a ladle to pour the chowder into two bowls. "If Mrs. Perkins is making this whole thing up, then why did a ghost show himself to me right near the restaurant lot? It would be too much of a coincidence."

"That's true." Viv added a bit of cream to the pan and stirred. When the mixture was warmed through, she spooned some onto each slice of bread and placed the slices on a platter. "More research needs to be done."

They carried the soup and bread and salad out to the table on the deck where Viv lit the jar candles and the cousins sat down to eat. The dog and cat went down the steps where they settled on the grass to guard the yard against chipmunks and squirrels.

Viv sipped from her wine glass. "You said the new ghost and the workmen ghosts were dressed in clothes that looked like fashion from the early nineteen-hundreds."

Lin nodded as she took a bite of the bread Viv had made. She closed her eyes as she chewed. "This is delicious."

"So what was going on in town at that time?"

"Well," Lin said, "Prohibition was in force in the whole country back then. The on-island economy had improved due to tourism. I can't think of anything else." Lifting her spoon, she sampled the corn chowder and gave Viv an appreciative look. "I wonder what the building that houses the inn-restaurant used to be. We should go to the museum and see if we can find out the history on that building. That could tell us what the place was used for in the early nineteen-hundreds."

"Good idea. Maybe that will explain what the men are loading and hauling around in that lot." Viv passed the platter of bread slices to Lin. "You told me that Mrs. Perkins's family has owned those two houses on Fairview Street for decades. Maybe we could look into that and see if there's any connection between who lived in the houses and what was in the other building."

"Anton might be able to help us." Lin spooned the last bit of soup into her mouth. "I'll talk to him tomorrow." Looking at her watch, she said, "Jeff and John will be here for dessert soon. We should clean up and I'll whip the cream."

"I need to warm the hot fudge, too." Viv and Lin had planned an ice cream sundae bar for the evening's dessert. Nicky glanced up and wagged his tail when he heard the word dessert.

The sun had set and fireflies could be seen flickering in the dark yard. A pleasant breeze fluttered over the deck now and then and rustled the leaves in the trees.

"Let's just sit for a few more minutes," Lin suggested. "It's such a beautiful evening."

Viv lifted her wine glass and eyed her cousin.

A Haunted Invitation

"Are you planning on ruining the night with a visit to Fairview Street later?"

Lin grinned. "Possibly."

"Maybe the guys will walk down there with us." Viv's voice was hopeful. Rubbing her forehead, she complained once again. "I really wish these ghosts weren't so puzzling. Why can't they just say what they want?"

"You know they don't work that way." A little sigh slipped from Lin's lips.

"Maybe you should have a talk with them."

Lin smiled. "They don't talk to me, remember."

"Well, maybe you could talk to them. Tell them what we need in order to help out."

Lin reminded Viv what happened when she attempted to talk to a ghost. "That time I tried to talk to Sebastian, he just disappeared."

As Viv chattered on about how to get ghosts to be more forthcoming, a strange sensation washed over Lin and the breeze suddenly turned cold and chilled her skin. Lin's heart started to pound and she shifted her eyes towards the yard where she noticed Nicky and Queenie sitting at attention looking up at something that she couldn't see.

Slowly, a shimmering figure materialized in front of the animals. It was the ghost from Fairview Street. The man was dressed in a cap, white shirt, vest, and trousers. His face was expressionless, except for his eyes which bore into Lin's.

As the air around her body dropped nearly ten

degrees, Lin began to shiver and although she could hear Viv's voice, it seemed as if her cousin was speaking to her from inside a faraway tunnel. She could hear Viv call her name, but the ghost held her attention so strongly that she couldn't pull herself away in order to answer.

The ghost took a step forward. He held something in his hand. Extending his arm, he seemed to be offering it to Lin. She leaned forward slightly trying to see what it was.

Lin rose from her seat and as she did, Viv took hold of her arm. "What is it?"

The shimmering light emanating from the ghost grew brighter and Lin watched as the atoms began to swirl, faster and faster. "Wait," she called out. Before the word was out of her mouth, the ghost had disappeared.

Lin sank back onto her seat as Nicky and Queenie raced up the steps to the deck.

Viv stared at her cousin and gently placed her hand on Lin's shoulder. "Are you okay? Was it a ghost?"

Lin nodded causing her long brown hair to spill around her face. "It was the ghost from Fairview Street."

"What did he want?" Viv sat in the deck chair next to Lin.

Lin's face looked pale. "He held something in his hand. I think he was offering it to me."

Viv's eyebrows scrunched together. "What was

it?"

Lin shifted her eyes to Viv. "I think it was an invitation."

CHAPTER 8

"An invitation?" Viv's voice was loud and high-pitched and her eyes were like saucers as she placed her hand against her cheek. "An invitation to what?"

Shaking her head, Lin leaned back in her chair. "I have no idea." The visit from the ghost had left her weak and unsettled.

Nicky rubbed his head against his owner's leg and she reached down to pat him.

"What makes you think it was an invitation?" Viv frowned.

Lin bit her lip in thought. "It looked like a fancy envelope, cream-colored. The first thing that popped into my head was that he was handing me an invitation."

"Did he say anything to you?" Viv pressed her finger against her throbbing temple. "Did he communicate in any way?"

Rubbing her arms to ward off the chill that had overtaken her when the ghost appeared, Lin shook her head. "No, nothing."

A Haunted Invitation

Viv let out a groan. "As usual. That just emphasizes my complaint that these ghosts need to learn to speak."

Lin managed a chuckle. "Why don't you arrange a meeting with them?"

Ignoring her cousin's suggestion, Viv went on. "This whole thing makes me nervous."

"More than all the previous times?" Lin shrugged into the sweater that Viv had removed and handed to her.

"Yes, because of what we said earlier. You don't see the ghosts that Mrs. Perkins can see. I don't like it. Are they trying to trick you into something? Is this new ghost really working together with those workmen-ghosts to trick you somehow? Get you to do something?"

Lin raised an eyebrow. "That seems like kind of an elaborate plan."

"I feel uneasy." Viv wrapped her arms around herself.

Lin reached over and rubbed her cousin's back. "We'll be careful."

Viv looked at Lin with worry lines etched into her forehead. "Don't let anything happen to you."

Touching her finger to her horseshoe necklace, Lin felt a quiver of anxiety pulse through her veins. What did the ghost have in his hand? Was it really an invitation? If it was, then what was she being invited to? What did he want from her?

Lin stood up. "Let's go set up the ice cream

sundae bar. The guys will be here any minute." She lifted some of the dishes from the table and Viv pushed herself up and joined in clearing the deck table.

The rest of the evening went as planned without any ghosts making an appearance. The four young people made their sundaes and sat at Viv's dining table enjoying the ice cream, chatting, and laughing. Lin wanted to tell Jeff about the ghost and what seemed to be an invitation in his hand, but Viv's boyfriend, John, didn't know about Lin's special skill so she decided to wait until the next day to share the details of the evening visitation with Jeff.

While playing a board game together, John brought up the work on Mrs. Perkins's house. "I heard a glitch came up at the house on Fairview."

Jeff placed a few lettered tiles on the game board. "Yeah, I heard from Kurt earlier. Mrs. Perkins was not pleased about the delay in the renovations, so Kurt called in some favors from his plumbing contractor friend. The work that needs to be done will only push off the timeline for completion by a week."

"Lucky for Kurt and his business." John nodded. "Polly Perkins has a reputation. No one wants to get on her bad side."

Viv and Lin shared a look.

"What do you mean?" It was Viv's turn to play, but she didn't make a move to form a word on the game board. "What kind of a reputation does Mrs. Perkins have?"

Eager to hear John's reply, but not wanting to appear too interested, Lin pretended to move some of her lettered-tiles around on the wooden holder on the table in front of her.

"She's kind of a witch." John took a swallow from his glass of beer. "She's loaded to the gills, probably one of the wealthiest women on the island, or the mainland, for that matter."

"Really?" Lin looked up. "How did she make her money?"

"Well, she inherited some from her parents. She took their import-export business over and it took off. She invested in real estate and that took off as well." John groaned looking at the few options available on the game board. "Her husband owned an oil company before he died, but ole' Mrs. Perkins was the smart cookie in that family."

"What's her reputation?" Lin asked.

John reluctantly made his move on the board. "She does a lot of charity work and is known for her generosity, but in business? Look out. Shrewd, hard, mean. Mrs. Perkins gets what she wants and woe to anyone who gets in her way. I hear she's a lot like her father was."

"She didn't seem like that when I met her." Lin thought about her conversations with Mrs. Perkins and nothing she said or did suggested a hard-boiled business person. "She seemed kind of to-the-point, but not nasty or rude."

John smiled. "To-the-point is a good way to describe her. If you cross her, she'll get to the point all right. Actually, you'll get the point."

Viv frowned. "What does that even mean? You mean Mrs. Perkins would hurt someone?"

"Maybe not physically, but she'd basically ruin your business reputation. It would be hard to get any work if that old bat sullied your name." John took another swallow from his glass. "Rumors have swirled around that she put a number of people out of business, and over nothing, really. Somehow she felt they crossed her, she did her thing, and they lost their businesses."

"Come on," Viv scolded. "I don't believe it. How could she do that?"

Jeff and John leveled their eyes at Viv.

"Is that really true, do you think?" Lin wondered how much was rumor and how much was fact.

Jeff cleared his throat. "I wouldn't cross the woman."

"A few years ago, Mrs. Perkins worked with one of the Realtors in our office. A deal went sour and Mrs. Perkins was not pleased. I don't know what happened, but that Realtor quit and left for the mainland." John shook his head. "I wouldn't work with that woman no matter how much the commission might be." A corner of John's mouth turned up and he narrowed his eyes. "Or would I?"

His comment elicited chuckles around the table.

A Haunted Invitation

"You heard she's having an event at her house as soon as the renovations are completed?" John studied the board plotting his next move.

"Mrs. Perkins is having an event?" Lin asked.

John nodded. "It's a charity thing combined with a show-off her house type thing."

Jeff said, "Kurt told me she expects everyone who worked on the place to show up for the event." He looked at Lin. "You'll be expected to attend, too."

"Me?" Lin gulped. "But I'm just doing the yard."

Jeff nodded. "It's supposed to be all hands on deck."

"I wouldn't cross her, if I were you." John warned. "Do good work and do what she expects and you'll be golden. Otherwise, you'll be a leper and you'll lose all your clients."

Lin sat up, indignant. "I don't believe that."

"At your peril." John shrugged.

"We'll go together." Jeff smiled at Lin. "It might be fun."

"Are you invited?" Viv asked her boyfriend.

"Yup. The whole office is going." John winked at Viv. "Which means you're going, too." Moving a few tiles to his letter holder, he added, "Our engraved invitations will be arriving very soon."

Viv flashed her cousin a look as Lin's eyes widened and her jaw dropped slightly at the mention of the word, *invitation*.

***

The game ended with the four of them yawning and complaining about having to get up early the next day for work. Because of the late hour, the girls decided to postpone their return visit to Fairview Street for another evening and Lin decided to stay overnight with Viv because she was too lazy to leave the house and go home. While the girls were cleaning up, they discussed Mrs. Perkins and the invitation.

Viv put dishes in the dishwasher. "Mrs. Perkins sounds like a monster."

"I wonder though." Lin washed some pots in the sink. "A prominent business person attracts all kinds of comments and rumors. The woman is a good business person. People talk and exaggerate." Lin eyed her cousin with a grin and joked, "I've heard the exact same things about your business tactics."

Viv whirled, her eyes wide. "What? People say I'm a monster?"

Lin continued to tease. "You run a tight ship at your business. You know, unhappy customers, unhappy employees, they say negative things and talk spreads."

"Oh, no." Viv put her hand over her mouth.

Lin chuckled. "I'm teasing you. People only say good things about you. You and I are small fish business owners. We don't draw the attention that someone like Mrs. Perkins does."

Viv gave her cousin a scowl. "I don't know why I fall for anything you say."

Lin's face took on a serious expression. "What do you think about the invitation?"

Viv crossed her arms over her chest. "It could be a coincidence that John talked about Mrs. Perkins's invitation right after the ghost held one out to you."

Lin lowered her chin and looked up at her cousin with skepticism.

Viv batted at the air. "Oh, I know. When these ghosts are involved, there are no coincidences."

Lin took sheets for the guest bed out of the linen closet. "I guess we'll plan ahead and get new dresses then."

Viv cocked her head in a quizzical posture. "Why?"

Lin thought of the ghost's evening appearance and how he extended the envelope to her. "Because, we're going to be attending an event we were just invited to."

CHAPTER 9

As Lin knelt by the flower bed pulling out weeds, Anton and Libby Hartnett sat in lawn chairs listening to her story about last night's ghostly appearance. Whenever Lin moved to another section of the garden, Libby and Anton dragged their chairs across the lawn so they could continue to hear Lin's report about the ghosts.

The sun was high in the sky and the air carried some humidity causing Lin's sleeveless shirt to cling to her back. A drop of sweat traveled down her temple and she used the back of her hand to brush it away.

Anton paged through the book in his lap while Libby sat in the chair with her hands resting on the wooden arms. When Lin discussed Mrs. Perkins and what John said about her being hard driving and mean, Libby nodded her head slightly. "John isn't far off in his description. Polly Perkins has one desire … to accumulate wealth. She's ruthless in business. The woman has put many people out of business." Libby's eyes hardened. "Unnecessarily."

Looking over at Lin working in the flower bed, she warned, "Be careful around that woman, Carolin."

Lin turned and sat back on her heels. "Really? I'm just the gardener. Why would she bother with me?"

Libby's voice was forceful. "There's something about Polly Perkins that doesn't sit right with me."

"How do you mean?" Lin pulled her sun hat forward over her forehead to shade her eyes.

"For one, I think she's unethical." Libby smoothed her skirt. "I also think she can be dangerous. Let me modify that. I know she can be dangerous."

Lin eyed the older woman and absent-mindedly noticed that the heat never seemed to bother her. "Dangerous, how? In business? Does she take things too far? Must she win at all costs?"

"Yes." Libby wasn't giving much information for Lin to go on.

Narrowing her eyes, Lin made eye contact with Libby. "Dangerous? In what way is she dangerous? Is there something else besides putting people out of business?'

Libby's lips were pressed together in thin lines. "Possibly."

Lin had been puzzling over why the ghosts had showed themselves recently so she decided to move the conversation in a different direction. "Why do you think these ghosts have shown up now? From the way they're dressed, the ghosts look like they lived in the nineteen-hundreds. That's over a hundred years ago. Why visit now? What could have drawn them out?"

Libby glanced at Anton. "What do you think? Have you found any pertinent information?"

Anton pushed his black eyeglass frames up to the bridge of his nose. Lin was glad to see that he, too, was feeling the effects of the heat. The man was flushed from the warm temperatures and had little beads of sweat forming over his upper lip like a see-through mustache.

The historian sat straighter in his chair and cleared his throat. "I've found some information. The way the men's clothing was described tells me that they were probably living and working during Prohibition. I wouldn't be surprised if those ghost-men are loading bottles of alcohol into crates for shipping to the mainland, likely a job they performed during their lifetimes. During that period in history, the islands of Nantucket and Martha's Vineyard contributed to the movement, or smuggling, of alcohol. Ships lingered about ten miles from the islands, and acted as liquor "stores." That section of water was called "Rum Row." The gangs had short-wave radios on the island that were used to communicate with the ships. There was quite a bit of money to be made in smuggling. Actually, some impressive fortunes were made and the people making the money were very protective of their territory."

A Haunted Invitation

"I assume smuggling routes were well-protected by the gangs that thought they owned certain sections of the business?" Libby tapped her fingers together.

"Absolutely. From what I've read and researched, it could be nasty business." Anton was well-informed on any of the topics that involved the island and discussing the illegal business caused a look of alarm to wash over his face. "People lost their lives over the smuggling and trade of alcohol." He leaned forward. "Some were murdered to protect routes and to keep interlopers from horning in on someone else's territory." An involuntary shiver ran over the man's shoulders. "Nasty. Nasty behavior."

"So," Lin asked, "You think these ghost-men are actually involved with moving alcohol?"

"*Were* involved. Indeed, I do, yes." Anton removed his glasses and cleaned the lenses with the edge of his shirt. "Of course, I might be wrong," he sniffed.

Lin suppressed a giggle at Anton's farfetched suggestion that he would ever think he was wrong.

"Your idea about Prohibition and what the men are doing makes sense," Libby agreed. "The ghosts are going through the motions of the work they did years ago. They aren't preparing shipments of alcohol in the here and now. It's as if they are reliving a night of long ago, over and over."

"But, why? Why now?" Lin asked again. "Why

show up now?"

Libby looked down at Lin who sat in the grass with her little brown dog resting next to her and when she spoke her voice was gentle and kind. "I guess that is what you are going to find out." Libby's magnetic blue eyes were soft. "I'm very glad that you're on the island with us, Carolin." After a few moments, the woman checked her watch and stood up. "I have an appointment I must get to." She said her goodbyes to Lin and Anton and then started around the house to head to her car, but she stopped abruptly and turned back to Lin with a grave look on her face. "Be sure to always wear your necklace. There might be something about it that can help protect you."

Lin's mouth opened and formed the shape of an "O" while she watched Libby walk away. Flicking her eyes to Anton, she saw that his surprised expression matched her own. Lin protectively wrapped her fingers around her horseshoe pendant. "Why did she say that? She's never said that before."

Anton's eyebrows were raised. He shrugged. "I have no idea, but if I were you, I'd do what she suggests."

Lin tucked her necklace into the front of her tank top and went back to weeding the flowers. "Why can't I see those ghost-men? Why can Mrs. Perkins see them, but not me? What does it mean?"

Anton cradled the book on the Prohibition era in

his lap and turned to a different chapter. "How on earth would I know? You're the ghost expert, not me."

"Some expert," Lin muttered as she planted some new perennials in the bed. "Half the time, I don't even know what's going on. Make that ninety-nine percent of the time."

Anton kept his focus on the book. "Not knowing anything doesn't seem to interfere with your ability to get to the bottom of things."

"I wish the process was easier." Lin packed the soil around a new planting.

Nicky let out a loud woof causing Lin to jump and whip her head up just as a mass of cold air surrounded her. Turning her eyes in the direction the dog was facing, Lin saw the ghost from last night standing on Anton's deck staring at her. The intensity of his gaze caused Lin a moment of dizziness and she slipped back onto her butt. The ghost lifted his arm and pointed at her and a second later his form broke apart into a million shimmering atoms that swirled like a tornado until they disappeared.

Anton glanced at Lin who was still staring at the deck. "What's wrong with you?" He flashed his eyes to the deck and then turned back to Lin. "What's wrong with you?" Anton dropped the open book on the ground and hurried over to the young woman who sat on the lawn blinking across the yard at nothing. Placing his hand on her shoulder,

Anton's voice trembled a bit when he asked, "Was it a ghost?"

Lin gave a nod. "The new ghost. He was on the deck. He pointed at me."

Words poured out of Anton's mouth in a torrent. "Can I get you anything? A cold drink? Are you okay? What did he want? Did he say anything?"

Feeling drained, Lin managed a weak smile. "I'm okay. Will you sit with me for a minute?" She patted the grass next to her.

Anton nudged the book he was reading to the side with his foot and sat down on the ground beside Lin.

Sucking in a deep breath, Lin's eyes flicked to the book lying open on the grass in front of her. A photo of several men standing together caught her eye and caused her heart to skip a beat. She moved forward on her hands and knees to get a better look. Leaning close to the page, a gasp escaped from her throat.

Anton scurried over to her. "What's wrong?"

Lin pointed to the picture in the history book. Her index finger rested on the image of one of the men. "It's him."

Anton stared at the photograph. "Who?"

"Right here." Lin jabbed her finger against the page. "This man. It's him."

Lin's eyes bore into Anton's. "That man in the picture is my ghost."

A Haunted Invitation

CHAPTER 10

Anton and Lin stared at each other with wide eyes until Nicky woofed and shook them out of their amazement that the man in the photograph in Anton's history book was Lin's ghost.

"Are you sure?" Anton lifted the book from the lawn and peered at the photo. "Which one is he?"

Lin touched the picture gingerly. "I thought the ghost was pointing at me when he appeared, but he must have been pointing at this book."

Anton adjusted his glasses and read a few paragraphs. "The caption doesn't list individual names. The group of men was called the Rum Row Watch-Dogs."

Lin and Anton shared a quick glance before Anton returned his attention to the book. Reading the passages quickly, he summarized the information. "The Watch-Dogs were a group of private citizens who banded together to take turns patrolling the waters around the island to assist authorities in controlling the illegal movement of alcohol." Anton lifted his head and looked across the lawn to the deck off of his kitchen. "Hmm." He read another passage. "Citizen-groups could not make a dent in the illegal trade and members of these groups placed themselves at great risk in dealing with the organized gangs who profited from the activity, hence, many disbanded."

"My ghost was trying to help uphold the law." Lin took off her sun hat and placed it on the ground. She ran her hand over the damp strands of brown hair that stuck to her forehead. "Did my ghost get into trouble with the gangs?"

"Quite possibly." Anton pushed his short wiry, body off the lawn and took a few swipes at his bottom to remove the bits of grass that clung to his trousers.

Lin swallowed. "Did he get killed for interfering with the gangs?"

"There's a very good chance." Anton headed for the deck table that was shaded by an umbrella. "I must get out of this sun."

Nicky put his paws on Lin's lap and stretching his small body, swiped his tongue over his owner's cheek. Lin looked down at the dog. "How can I help this ghost? What does he want? How am I going to figure this out, Nick?"

The little brown dog rubbed his head against his owner and Lin pulled him close and wrapped him in a hug.

***

A Haunted Invitation

At the end of her work day, Lin decided to drive over to meet up with Leonard at his last client's home to go over some garden designs for a large job they had planned for next week. The sun was lower in the sky and a pleasant breeze had kicked up while Lin and Leonard sat in the back bed of Lin's truck eating slices of apple dipped in honey and peanut butter. The dog had no interest in what they were nibbling on so he rested quietly between them with his head on his front legs.

"Anton is researching the Prohibition era on the island." Lin dipped another slice into the little pot of honey she'd brought in the lunch bag.

"Why?" Leonard joked. "Does he feel the need to make alcohol illegal once again?"

Lin smiled. "He's doing it just for interest sake. You know how Anton can't get enough of the island's history. He found out that some of the citizens of the time joined forces to help the authorities police the waters to the southeast of Nantucket where illegal trading took place."

"Yeah, that area was called Rum Row." Leonard munched on a piece of apple. "It was noble of the citizens to get involved, but it was also pretty dumb of them."

Lin gave Leonard a look.

"Ordinary people up against armed gangs who would kill whoever got in their way?" The man shook his head. "Smuggling booze was big business, lots of money at stake. It's my understanding that those citizen policing groups disbanded pretty quickly. It only took a few of them getting killed for the others to high-tail it back to the harbor and quit the idea of monitoring the illegal activity."

"How do you know this stuff?" Lin licked a bit of peanut butter off of her finger.

"My wife had a relative involved."

"On which side?" Lin questioned.

"The watch-dog side."

Nicky raised his head at the word 'dog' and Leonard gave him a scratch behind the ears. "Marguerite kept some old newspaper articles that had been handed down from her grandparents. I'll see if I can find them if you think Anton would be interested."

Excitement caused Lin's heart to skip a beat. "Oh, I bet he'd love to see them. So would I." Lin couldn't reveal the real reason she wanted to read the newspaper stories about the watch-dog groups during Prohibition, so she said, "I love reading about the island's history."

"I think the box is still in the attic. I'll see about digging them out."

"The citizens must have known how dangerous it was trying to prevent the alcohol smuggling." Lin ran her hand over Nicky's back. "Why would they even attempt it?"

Leonard shrugged a shoulder. "Adventure, moral inclination, a sense of importance. People get involved in dangerous things for any number of reasons."

Lin narrowed her eyes. "Which side would you have been on?"

Leonard raised an eyebrow and smiled. "The smuggling side, of course. I wouldn't mind some financial security."

Lin gave the man a playful poke with her elbow. "I bet you wouldn't have."

"Who knows what you'll do until you're in the actual situation."

"Did Marguerite's relative stay involved long?"

Leonard's voice was matter-of-fact. "No. He got killed."

"Oh, gosh, he did?" The thought that her ghost might be related to Marguerite flashed in Lin's head. "What was his name? Do you know what he looked like?"

"Denton Mullins was his name. He was a minister at one of the churches here. He was a small guy, round in the middle, bald."

Lin breathed a sigh. Marguerite's relative didn't match her ghost's description. "He must have thought he was protecting his congregation."

"From reading the stories, Marguerite had the impression that Minister Mullins didn't know the first thing about boating, but he blustered his way into the watch-dog group. The smugglers didn't kill him. He fell overboard while out on patrol one night. Besides being ignorant about boating, it seems the good minister couldn't swim either."

Lin groaned.

Leonard took a swig from his water bottle. "The man would have done better to stay in the pulpit."

After a few minutes, Lin brought up Mrs. Perkins. "It turns out that I'm expected to attend an event at Mrs. Perkins's mansion after the renovations are complete. I should have made you do the work there then you would be the one who has to go, not me."

"Don't go if you don't want to."

"It is expected. John said not to cross the woman. I guess she has a reputation."

"I've heard." Leonard nodded. "Who knows which parts are true and which parts are rumor."

"Libby also told me not to cross her."

"Well, that's probably good advice when dealing with just about anyone." Leonard poured some water into his palm and splashed it on his face.

"Have you heard bad things about Mrs. Perkins? Is she dangerous?"

Leonard wiped his wet palm on his jeans. "I've heard she's put some people out of business. I've also heard she had a man killed for trying to cheat her."

"What?" Lin almost shouted.

"No charges were ever filed. The whole thing could have been an exaggeration."

"How do you exaggerate getting killed?" Lin's eyes widened like saucers. "Either he got killed or he didn't. You're either dead or you're alive. There isn't anything in between."

"I meant that rumors fly. The story could have been made up."

Lin's shoulders sagged and she half-joked. "So just in case, I'd better go to the party and not cross Mrs. Perkins."

"That might be for the best." Leonard grinned.

Lin looked at her landscaping partner out of the corner of her eye. "You're an equal partner in this business. Want to go to the event with me?"

"Nope." Leonard jumped off the back of the truck. "Time to head home."

Nicky stood for his final patting of the day from Leonard.

The tall man looked at Lin. "Just in case, be careful around that woman, Coffin."

Alarm shot through Lin's body. "Why are you saying that?"

Leonard gave a shrug and headed for his own truck. "Don't be like those Prohibition watch-dogs nosing around in stuff they shouldn't be nosing around in. Self- preservation, that's the number one rule."

Leonard got into his truck and, with a wave of his hand, he backed out of the client's driveway and drove away leaving Lin standing beside her vehicle, her mind rehashing the two warnings she'd received in one day and wondering how on Earth she was going to figure out what her ghost wanted from her and how she'd ever be able to help him.

CHAPTER 11

Lin and Viv parked their bicycles in the bike rack and followed the sandy path past green bushes and fragrant rosa rugosa down the hill to Steps white sand beach. The azure ocean stretched out before them under the bright blue sky and the cousins couldn't wait to get into the water.

Unzipping their backpacks, they took out towels and spread them on the warm sand. Just before they pulled off their shorts and tank tops and raced each other into the sea, Lin reached for her pendant necklace thinking she should remove it for safekeeping. Her fingers were just about to undo the clasp when Libby's words rang in her head. *Be sure not to remove your necklace.* Lin left the pendant around her neck.

The cousins swam and dove and floated in the refreshing water for over an hour under the hot sun before returning to the beach to dry off.

"This was a great idea." Lin removed her lunch container from her backpack and nibbled on her sandwich. Viv had suggested a late afternoon trip to the beach and Lin worked like a wild woman until 2pm to get most of her clients' work done in order to meet Viv for the late lunch beside the water. "We need to do more of this."

Viv finished her yogurt and placed the empty container back into her backpack. Both young women smoothed out the towels and rested on their backs to soak up some sun.

"Tell me more about the picture of the ghost in the history book and what Anton and Leonard told you." Viv rubbed some sunscreen on her arms.

Lin recapped what she'd learned. "I thought the ghost was pointing to me, but it turns out he was indicating the history book. He wanted us to find his picture in the book."

"Too bad their names weren't listed in the caption." Viv put on her sunglasses. "It would be a bit more information to go on."

After more discussion about the ghost, the ghost-men, the rum runners and the danger in trying to curb the smugglers' illegal activities, Viv bolted up into sitting position. "For Pete's sake."

Lin lifted her head and shaded her eyes. "What's wrong with you?"

"I own a bookstore. There's an entire section of books on the island's history including the Prohibition era. We need to look at those books when we get back."

"Right in front of us." Lin grinned. "How will we help the ghost if we miss things that are right under our noses?" Shaking her head, Lin added, "This new ghost may want to rethink who he's asking for assistance."

When their swimsuits were fully dry, they packed their things into the backpacks and headed up the sandy hill.

"Going up is a lot harder than coming down." Although she loved being outside biking on the pathways around the island and swimming in the ocean, Viv wasn't much for exercising in the heat and preferred the comfort of an air conditioned room. "Carry me."

Lin smiled and took Viv's backpack from her to lighten her load. "How's that?"

"Much better, but now I feel guilty."

Chuckling, Lin held Viv's backpack out to her. "Want it back?"

"I don't feel that guilty." The sunlight caused the gold highlights in Viv's light brown hair to sparkle like the bright tones of her laugh.

Glancing at the beautiful seascape stretching out behind them, Lin thought about the rum runners and how some of them committed murder to keep hold of their smuggling routes. She shook her head in disgust at how greed could trump consideration for life and caring about a fellow human being. The rumors and what people thought about Mrs. Perkins popped into Lin's head and if what was said about the woman was true, then she wasn't much different than the rum runners.

"On the way back, would you take a detour with me?" Lin unlocked her bike and tugged on the cord that ran through hers and Viv's tires.

"Where to?" Viv shrugged on her backpack and straddled her bicycle.

"I'd like to swing by the restaurant next to the lot where the ghost-men were working." Lin climbed onto her bike. "I think we should talk to the owner."

***

The cousins locked their bikes around the base of a streetlamp's post and headed into the restaurant to ask for the manager or owner. The place was buzzing with workers preparing for the evening customers. Viv and Lin had never eaten at the fancy establishment and the two admired the soft lighting, tables covered with white linen cloths, and the polished wood of the bar.

A tall, slim man with blonde hair cut close to his head hurried over. He wore a slim-fitting starched white dress shirt and tailored black trousers. "May I help you?"

Lin introduced themselves. "Sorry to bother. I know you're getting ready for the first dinner seating. We had a question about some activity that went on behind the restaurant a few evenings ago."

A frown formed on the owner's face and he gestured for Lin and Viv to sit with him at one of the tables. "I've had a complaint recently about that very thing. Are you related to the woman who made the original complaint?"

"Not at all," Viv told the owner.

"You heard the noise? You saw the workers?"

Lin shook her head. "We only heard about it." Fibbing, she told the man, "A friend of ours is looking to buy in the area and had some worries about the supposed noise. She asked if we'd drop by and find out what the story was."

The owner looked relieved. "I honestly don't know anything about it. I wondered if the previous complaint was valid since none of the other neighbors have voiced concerns. I'm glad to hear that you haven't been bothered by the alleged situation."

"Why do you say 'alleged'?" Viv questioned.

"The person who made the complaint told me that she saw and heard a great deal of activity behind the restaurant on two occasions. I don't have any idea what she was talking about. If there was activity in the lot, it has nothing to do with my establishment."

"There haven't been any other complaints?" Lin asked.

"Nothing. Just the one time, from the one person." The owner looked quite offended by the accusation of causing a nighttime disturbance. "I work very hard to be a good neighbor. We don't stay open late. We're only open for dinner."

"Perhaps the complaint was unfounded?" Viv suggested.

The owner stiffened. "I'm not sure." He adjusted the silverware next to the plate in front of him. "I stayed overnight here two evenings after receiving the complaint. I wanted to catch whoever was responsible."

"And?" Lin raised an eyebrow.

"Nothing." The man's posture was ramrod straight. "I stayed awake both nights. Nothing happened. No one was back there."

"That was very nice of you to do that." Viv was impressed that the hardworking man would stay up two nights in a row to find out what was bothering his neighbors.

"I was concerned about the disturbance, of course. As I said, I try to be a good neighbor." The owner took a quick glance over his shoulder. "But there was another reason for my worry."

A shiver ran down Lin's back.

"What was it?" Viv leaned forward.

"The woman who made the complaint did so in person. When I told her I didn't know what she was talking about, she became angry. She thought I was lying to her." The man lowered his voice. "The woman told me that she'd only recently moved into her house on Fairview Street from across the island and wouldn't stand for a noisy, disruptive neighborhood." He paused for a moment. "If I didn't get to the bottom of the late night commotion, the woman threatened to damage my business." Making eye contact with Lin and Viv, he added, "I believed her."

***

"Well, heck." Viv's eyes flashed. "That old cow can't go around threatening people because things aren't to her liking."

The cousins walked their bikes around the corner from the restaurant. Lin glanced around worriedly. "Keep your voice down. Mrs. Perkins could be walking around here. And I guess she can and does go around making threats."

"It's terrible." Viv scowled. "Can't anything be done about her?"

Letting out a sigh, Lin said, "Maybe she just tries to intimidate people to frighten them. Maybe she never carries out her threats."

Viv grunted. "She makes me sick."

"Let's forget about her for now." Lin touched her pendant necklace absent-mindedly. "Come on. Let's go to the bookstore and take a look at those history books you have in stock." Lin swung her leg over her bike. "That conversation made me anxious and unsettled. I'd like to get away from here for a while."

Viv looked across the street of the tree-lined neighborhood towards Mrs. Perkins's mansion. "I don't think you're going to get your wish."

"What?" Lin followed Viv's gaze and saw Jeff standing on the front steps of the Georgian-style brick mansion under renovation. He was waving the young women over.

Letting out a low groan, Lin led her cousin to the viper's nest.

A Haunted Invitation

CHAPTER 12

Jeff greeted the two cousins by giving Viv a hug and Lin a kiss. "Come in and see the renovations."

Lin eyed the front door warily. "I don't think we should come in."

"It's fine. No one's here except the workers." Jeff opened the front door. "Mrs. Perkins and her friend went to Boston overnight yesterday. They won't be back until later today. The rooms are coming out great. I thought you'd like to see what's been done."

They stepped into a perfectly decorated foyer with a carved wooden staircase standing before them. An antique chest was placed on one wall and above it hung an oil painting of a sailing sloop. A small cut-glass chandelier lit the space.

"It's beautiful," Viv murmured.

"These front rooms haven't been touched. The renovations are being done at the back of the property." Jeff led the way down a hall past several living areas. Lin and Viv peeked in as they passed. One room was set up as a living area with cream-colored sofas and chairs placed around a cherrywood coffee table. A wood-burning fireplace with a marble surround stood on the far wall and rugs of cream and cranberry covered the polished wood floors. The living room led into a sitting room decorated in much the same way. A sparkling crystal chandelier hung from the coffered ceiling.

They passed a dining room with a mahogany table and twelve chairs set on a crimson and rose rug. One wall of the room had been painted with a scene of a sail boat heading away from Nantucket town.

"Gosh," Viv whispered. "Who knew these homes were so elaborate."

Entering the back of the house into an enormous kitchen, Jeff introduced Lin and Viv to the workers. The renovated kitchen sported high-end white cabinetry, a six-burner stainless steel stove, and a built-in refrigerator-freezer. Glossy slabs of granite topped a huge center island and the cabinet counters. To the right, the kitchen opened to a large family room-sitting area with tall windows looking out over the manicured grounds. Cut-glass vases held arrangements of fresh flowers and a slight floral scent wafted on the air.

Lin stepped to the floor-to-ceiling window. "Yikes. I didn't realize how large the back gardens of these homes were. It's like a park out there. I've only seen the front and side yards of this house. I had no idea this was behind the fence." A circular brick patio was ringed with flowering hydrangea bushes and an arched trellis covered with pink roses led to the grassy area. At the rear, a white gazebo sat perched next to another brick patio with gardens all around it. "How much money does this woman have?" Lin's jaw had dropped.

Jeff chuckled. "Plenty." He led the young women through a few more of the rooms to show them the beautiful work done by Kurt's crew. "There are twenty rooms in the house. The place was built in 1855 by a prominent businessman. There's a cupola on the roof big enough for four people to stand in and downstairs there's a wine cellar, wine tasting room, full kitchen, media room, small dining room, two bathrooms and a bedroom. The doors down there have direct access to the outside patio."

When Jeff was describing the lower level of the mansion, Lin started to feel anxious. She rubbed her bare arms. "It's very cold in here."

Both Jeff and Viv gave Lin a look.

"It's not cold in here at all. It's comfortable." Viv stepped closer to her cousin and glanced nervously around the space. "Do you see anything?"

A flurry of nervous energy flooded Lin's body. "No."

"Do you want to go on with the tour or would you rather not?" Jeff asked.

Lin swallowed hard and nodded. "Let's go on."

Giving Jeff a little smile, she tried to reassure her companions that everything was fine even though her skin felt prickly and her heart was pounding like a drum as she followed Jeff and Viv through the rooms.

Lin tried to focus her attention on the lovely renovation work that was nearly complete, but something kept picking at her creating two different sensations ... one moment, she had the urge to flee the home and the next second, she had the feeling that she was supposed to stay and help someone in need. Despite feeling freezing cold, little beads of sweat formed on Lin's forehead.

Jeff stepped to a staircase. "This leads to the lower level."

Putting her foot on the top step, Lin's throat began to constrict and she coughed trying to open it, but the tissues continued to tighten. Just as Lin's hand flew to her throat and she began to gasp, she had the impression of someone rushing by at the bottom of the staircase.

Thinking that Lin needed fresh air, Jeff grabbed her hand and pulled her through the rooms to the outside loggia that overlooked the grounds. Lin sank onto one of the soft cushioned chairs and in between sucking in long, deep breaths, she attempted to smile to alleviate Jeff's and Viv's concern. "I'm okay," she squeaked. "It must have been an allergic reaction to some paint or glue or something that one of the workmen was using."

Jeff kneeled in front of his girlfriend. He gave Viv a quick glance.

"I think it was something other than a reaction to some substance." Viv pushed her bangs to the side and sat down next to Lin. "You aren't allergic to anything."

Lin's breathing was slowly returning to normal.

Jeff held her hand. "Can I get you a drink? A blanket?"

"I'm okay now." She nodded at Jeff.

"It was a ghost, wasn't it?" Viv leveled her eyes at her cousin.

Lin's shoulders shrugged. "I don't know what it was. I thought I saw someone rush by at the bottom of the stairs. It frightened me."

"Maybe it was some nervousness over being in the house," Jeff suggested. "You've heard some unpleasant things about Mrs. Perkins. Maybe you were upset about what you'd heard about her combined with being inside her house."

"Maybe that was it." Trying to lighten the atmosphere of worry surrounding them, Lin said, "It's good I was inside the house before attending that party she's going to throw. I wouldn't want to faint or whatever during the event." She gave a weak, little chuckle. "Now I can be ready for any odd sensation that decides to descend on me."

After sitting and talking for fifteen minutes, they all walked back into the house and down the hall to the front door. Standing under the portico, Jeff hugged his sweetheart and the girls left the mansion and unlocked their bikes from the streetlamp post.

"It was a ghost, wasn't it?" Viv asked again.

"I think it was, even though I didn't really see anyone. It was more of an impression, a feeling." Lin put the bike lock into her backpack. "I've never felt that sensation before. It felt like a mix of danger and sadness and needing help." Lin shivered recalling the feeling. "I felt panicky and I didn't know what to do. As we started down to the lower level, I started to feel like I couldn't breathe, then I felt that someone was there. I panicked."

"It must have been a ghost. Maybe it's a ghost who is too shy to show itself to you." Viv took hold of the bike's handlebars and started walking the bicycle up the cobblestone road. "Maybe it needs something from you, but can't bring itself to make an appearance."

"I wonder. Usually ghosts show themselves to me before I feel the need to help." Lin thought about what her cousin said about the ghost being shy as the two walked down the quiet side street. "I hope Jeff doesn't think I'm a nut."

The corners of Viv's mouth turned up. "Well, it would be hard not to think such a thing about you."

Lin didn't respond to her cousin's comment. She couldn't imagine why a ghost would hide from her if it needed or wanted something. Thinking about how she'd felt inside Mrs. Perkins's house made her shudder. "I'm not looking forward to going back inside that house."

"Don't worry. We'll all be with you at the party." Viv turned her bike onto another quiet street that led to the side of the building that housed her bookstore. She gave Lin a wink. "You know, it might even liven up the event if you do pass out when you're there."

Lin scowled. "Thanks a lot."

CHAPTER 13

Inside Viv's bookstore, Lin followed her cousin to the history section of the book shelves and gathered several of the volumes on Nantucket. They carried them to a nearby table and began poring over the pages looking for any information on the citizen watch-dog groups that had formed to combat the illegal smuggling of alcohol during Prohibition. Viv's employee, Mallory, brought them lattes and muffins and they eagerly bit into the sweets.

"I'm starving." Lin put a piece of the toasted and buttered blueberry muffin into her mouth. "Yum. So good."

After thirty minutes of reading, Viv closed the book she'd been searching through. "Nothing much in this one either. There's just a basic mention of the citizen groups with no details to help us."

"It's the same with this one." Lin slid the paperback into the pile of books they'd already checked over. "Maybe we need to visit the historical museum and have a look at their collection."

"It wouldn't hurt." Viv sighed. "What's with this new ghost? He's only shown up a few times. He's not assisting much at all. Maybe he doesn't want you to help him with anything."

"That's not the impression I get. It's not the feeling I get either. He's full of sadness. I know he wants something." Lin put her elbow on the table and rested her chin in her hand. "He wants me to do something. I just haven't figured out what it is yet."

Viv's regal gray cat, Queenie, strolled over to the table and jumped up onto Lin's lap. She stood up and put her front paws against Lin's chest causing the young woman to laugh. "What's with you, Queenie? You want something from me, too?"

The cat leapt onto the floor and strode away to the shelf where the girls had removed some of the history books. The cat glanced back at Lin, paused, and then sauntered back to her upholstered chair where she jumped up onto the cushion and curled into a tight ball for a nap.

Lin and Viv exchanged a look.

"What's up with the cat?" Lin asked. "She's never done that before."

Viv got up to check the other books on the shelf. Placing her hand on her hip, she bent and scanned the titles. "There isn't anything else here that could be of interest. We took every book on the history of Nantucket."

"Queenie must be playing with us." Lin finished

off her muffin and thought about the day's events. "Why do you think I had such a strong reaction in Mrs. Perkins's house? Was it ghost-related or was it because of all the awful things we've heard about her?"

Viv sank into the chair opposite Lin. "I don't know. It must be partially ghost-related. You've never reacted that way before. It might just be a combination of everything, although, there are some puzzling aspects to this situation." Viv pursed her lips in thought and then lifted one of her fingers for each point she made. "One, you can't see the ghosts that Mrs. Perkins can see. Two, you had those strong feelings in her house. And three, Libby told you not to take off your necklace." Viv stared at her cousin. "Guess what?" She paused for effect. "I don't like it."

Lin grinned. Viv never liked anything that had to do with ghosts. "I've been turning all of those things over in my mind."

"And?"

Lin held her hands up in a helpless gesture.

"Great. So what's the next step?" Viv sipped from her cup. "We head to the historical museum or just forget about the whole thing?" Viv gathered the used cups and dessert plates from the table. "Don't answer. I know what you'll say."

Two customers walked by chattering with each other and Viv looked over at them. A surprised expression played across the young woman's face as her eyes widened. Lin followed her cousin's gaze and when she saw the customers, her throat tightened for a moment and she had to swallow hard.

"Oh, look who it is." Polly Perkins advanced on Lin's table with her friend right on her heels. The woman wore a pale blue expensive-looking tailored summer dress with carefully chosen jewelry. Her white-blonde hair was perfectly styled. "We just returned from Boston." Mrs. Perkins gestured at her friend. "Linda needs some paperbacks to read. I haven't read a thing in ages." Mrs. Perkins sounded proud of her book avoidance. "I'm just too busy. Maybe someday I'll have the necessary leisure time to indulge in frivolous activities like reading things someone makes up."

The friend looked slightly offended by Polly Perkins's dismissive remarks about reading, but she stayed silent and didn't attempt to defend herself against the put-down. Lin could see that Viv was steaming at the comments, but she knew her cousin would remain tactful despite wanting to counter Mrs. Perkins's rude words.

Mrs. Perkins looked directly at Viv. "You deal in such things. What recommendations do you have for Linda?"

Viv and Lin both wondered why Linda McQueen couldn't speak for herself and why she would ever have chosen such an overbearing friend.

Viv walked past Mrs. Perkins brusquely and

spoke directly to Linda. "What do you enjoy reading?" The two walked away towards the fiction section of the bookstore.

Mrs. Perkins looked after them for a moment and deciding not to follow, turned to Lin and spoke with a demanding tone to her voice. "How are my front and side gardens coming along?"

Lin didn't care to be looked down on by the woman so she stood up in order to be at eye level with Mrs. Perkins. "They're looking very nice. I should be done in two days."

Mrs. Perkins huffed. "Such small spaces. I'd thought you'd be finished by now."

"Often the smallest spaces need the most attention," Lin countered.

"Hmm. Is that so?" The woman glanced around with a bored expression. "I'll go see what's keeping Linda. I need to get home."

Sitting back in her chair, Lin could feel the anger percolating inside of her and she wished she didn't have to deal with such self-absorbed people. Waiting for Viv to return, she tried to shake off her annoyance.

A sudden sense of exhaustion pushed down on Lin from the combination of the afternoon's sunning and swimming, being overcome at Mrs. Perkins's house with alarming feelings, and now having to listen to the tyrannical woman's unpleasant yammering. She felt like rushing home and falling asleep on the sofa with her sweet little dog.

Lin yawned and as she was about to push up from the table, a shaft of freezing air engulfed her with such speed that her breath caught in her throat. She lifted her eyes to the aisle between the bookshelves and saw the shimmering form of her ghost staring at her. The spirit's body seemed to brighten and fade as if he was having trouble making his appearance. Worried that he might evaporate, Lin tried to push everything out of her mind so that she was open to whatever might float on the air to her from the ghost.

The spirit's eyes seemed to fill with tears and his form showed signs of losing its luster. Lin was sure he would disappear before giving her a clue to what he needed, but just as some of his atoms seemed to spark and flare, he turned and looked up at the higher shelf. As he reached his hand out to Lin, the particles of his body popped and sizzled, and then he was gone.

The cold air surrounding Lin was sucked away in an instant and her body began to warm. She felt almost like all of her energy had been sucked away with the freezing air and she stood blinking at the spot where the ghost had stood.

Viv buzzed around the corner. "Those two are gone, thank heavens. What a weird relationship, one is a bossy witch and the other is a passive wimp. I'd be happy if I never ran into either one of them ever again." Viv noticed the weird way her cousin was standing and hurried over to her. "What happened? Did he show up?"

Lin nodded. Her pale face turned to Viv. "He pointed to the upper shelf."

Viv took Lin by the arm and steered her to the bookshelf where they both peered up at the books on the next-to-top shelf. "There." Viv stood on tiptoes and took a book down. "Someone misfiled this book." She handed it to Lin. "Let's have a look."

Sitting shoulder-to-shoulder, the two slowly turned the pages scanning each one for any pertinent information.

"Look." Viv's voice was excited. "Here are some details on the watch-dog groups."

They read the passages together and then turned the page.

What she saw in the book caused Lin to jerk backwards and suck in a breath. "Look, Viv. There he is." She placed her index finger under one of the black and white photographs showing several men standing together.

Viv read the caption. "The men's names are listed." She ran her finger over the words. "Here it is. His name is here." Her voice bubbled with excitement. "His name is William Weston." Viv turned her eyes to Lin and smiled. "That's your man."

A Haunted Invitation

CHAPTER 14

Lin, Viv, and Jeff sat under the stars sipping Jeff's homemade sangria on the deck of John's boat docked in Nantucket town's harbor. The heat and humidity of the day had been swept away by a soft lovely breeze off the ocean. Jeff had made a variety of appetizers and set them on the table in the center of the chairs so everyone could reach. Lin put a few mini pizzas on a small plate and dug into them. Viv reached for the small squares of spanakopita while Jeff chose a couple of quiche rounds and slices of grilled sausage. John sat next to Viv and he filled his plate with some of everything.

Lin was feeling much better than she had when she'd visited Mrs. Perkins's mansion in the late afternoon. After learning the name of her ghost at Viv's bookstore, she went home for a nap and a shower and felt rejuvenated and eager to join her cousin and friends on the boat, despite the late hour. Candles flickered in little jars set around the boat deck illuminating the shadows and creating a pretty atmosphere.

Balancing her plate on her lap, Lin leaned back in her chair for a moment and let out a contented sigh. "This is just what I needed."

"I agree." Viv sipped her fruity drink and watched the tourists strolling by on the docks. "We should do this every night ... especially after such a weird day."

"What happened? Why was it weird?" John asked as he reached for more appetizers.

Viv told her boyfriend about their visit to Mrs. Perkins's mansion and how Lin felt very uncomfortable there and seemed to have an allergic reaction to something in the house. John didn't know about Lin's "gifts" so Viv had to attribute her cousin's feelings of discomfort and alarm to something other than ghosts. Viv also relayed the tale of Mrs. Perkins and Mrs. McQueen's shopping trip to the bookstore and she did not mince words about what a hag Mrs. Perkins was. "Honestly, that woman. She's a self-absorbed, overbearing witch. Why Mrs. McQueen puts up with that pompous windbag, I have no idea."

John popped a mini quiche round into his mouth and mumbled, "Tell us what you really think about her."

Viv shook her head. "I'm not saying anything that any person who has ever met that woman wouldn't say."

Lin was dying to tell Jeff that they'd discovered the name of her ghost, but the news would have to wait until the next day since Jeff had to leave the boat in order to give his sister a lift from town to her house about fifteen minutes away. He gave Lin a kiss and a hug and wished everyone a good night as he headed off the deck and walked away down the docks to his truck.

The conversation turned to the upcoming town festival and Viv talked about running a sidewalk sale at the bookstore the weekend of the festival like she'd done early in the summer. "It was a big success when I did it a couple of months ago." She smiled sweetly at John. "I just need someone with strong arms to help us move the books outside."

"I wonder where you'll find someone like that," John teased.

Just as the girls were finishing their drinks and preparing to head to their homes, John's phone buzzed with a text and he reached for it and looked at the screen. "Huh."

Viv asked what the message was about.

John leaned forward. "It's my buddy at the police station. He says that the pompous windbag, as she's known to you," he glanced at Viv, "has just called the station with a complaint and wants a cruiser sent over to her street."

"What's the complaint?" Lin questioned.

"The usual." John placed his phone on the table. "Noise and commotion behind the Founders Inn and Restaurant."

Lin and Viv shared a quick look.

"Interesting." Viv looked at her watch. "Well, I guess we should call it a night. Tomorrow is another early day."

"As always." Lin stood up and helped gather the dishes and glasses to take below. When she returned to the deck, Lin thanked John for the nice evening and Viv and John shared a kiss before the girls left the boat for the walk home.

"Care to make a detour?" Viv raised an eyebrow.

"You bet I would."

Viv and Lin quickened their pace and weaved around late-night restaurant and bar goers as they made their way up the brick sidewalks of Main Street under the shining streetlamps and took the second turn onto Fairview Street.

"Do you think you'll see anything?" Viv asked.

Lin's heart beat sped up the closer they got to their destination. "Maybe. Maybe not."

"Let's hug the shadows." Viv edged closer to the side of the walkway so as not to be directly under the streetlights.

The cousins slowed as they approached the back of the restaurant building.

"I don't hear anything." Viv stopped and listened.

"Let's get closer." Lin maneuvered nearer to the lot and when she had a good line of sight, she shrugged. "It's empty. No one's here."

Viv groaned. "Is that woman just dreaming the noise and movement and then calling the police?"

A Haunted Invitation

"I don't think so." Lin eyed the area, afraid of what she might see.

The cousins walked through the lot to peek into the small ditch that ran along the side of the space where Mrs. Perkins claimed the workers had hidden from the police on previous nights. The ditch was as empty as the lot.

A shaft of bright light shined on the girls and they both jumped and wheeled around. An officer called to them. Lin shaded her eyes from the flashlight and spotted a police cruiser parked at the curb.

"What are you doing there?" the officer called.

"We're cutting through the lot on our way home." Viv took a few steps towards the man.

Another officer came up behind the first and the girls were questioned briefly. "You didn't see any guys around here making a bunch of noise?"

"Nothing. No one was here." Lin gestured to the street that ran off of Fairview. "We were at the docks earlier and now we're heading home. We didn't see anyone here in the lot when we came through."

The first officer let out a grunt. "Another false alarm. Sorry to bother you." The men returned to the cruiser and drove away.

Lin and Viv shook their heads and walked out of the lot on their way to the side street that they would follow to get to their homes. As they passed by the house where Mrs. Perkins was staying during renovations on her mansion, a voice called from the upper floor window. "Is that you, Lin Coffin?"

Lin's heart rate doubled. Looking up, she saw Mrs. Perkins, the woman's hair a bit askew, leaning out of the window wearing a fluffy robe.

"Did you see the men working in that lot?" Mrs. Perkins demanded.

"No." Lin stared up at the woman. "We're just walking home. We've only been in the area for a minute."

They heard Mrs. Perkins let out a few choice curses. "Where did those men run off to?" She pulled her head back inside and stepped further into the room. The girls could see the woman walking away from the window.

Lin stared at the upper floor for a few seconds and then she shrugged. "I guess Mrs. Perkins is done questioning us."

Viv took hold of Lin's arm. "Let's get out of here before she decides to continue the interrogation." The two scurried away and turned at the corner. "She thinks she sees men working back there." Viv puffed a bit as they walked up the slight hill. "Why on earth can she see the ghosts, but no one else can?"

An odd sensation of being watched came over Lin as a wave of familiar cool air surrounded her. She stopped short and slowly turned around to look back down the road.

Several blocks away, Lin's translucent ghost

stood at the corner under the golden glow of a streetlamp. He made eye contact with the young woman and bits and pieces of ideas and thoughts swirled in Lin's head and nearly came together to supply the answers she needed, but then they cartwheeled away before she could grasp them.

The ghost seemed to weaken from his attempt at silent communication with Lin and she watched with regret as his form grew fainter and fainter and then disappeared.

"It was William Weston." Hoping he would reappear, Lin gazed at the spot where the ghost had stood. "He was standing down there watching us. He's gone now."

"Did he tell you something?" Peering down the road, Viv moved a little closer to Lin.

"I think he did." Lin gave her cousin a puzzled look. "I just don't know what it was."

CHAPTER 15

Toweling off her hair from the shower, Lin crossed the kitchen barefoot to remove a can of seltzer from the refrigerator. Pulling the tab on the top of the can, a little whoosh of air was released. The front doorbell rang as Lin took a long sip of the cold liquid. While Nicky woofed and took off for the door to see who had come for a visit, Lin peeked out the front window to see Leonard's truck parked at the curb.

When she opened the door, the little brown dog performed his welcoming dance around the big man until Leonard laughed and bent to scratch the animal's chin. Tucked under his right arm, Lin's business partner carried a rectangular brown box tied up with string.

"Here are those old newspaper articles that Marguerite saved about her ancestors." Leonard walked through the living room into the kitchen and placed the box on the island. "It smells good in here."

"There's a shepherd's pie in the oven. Viv's

coming for dinner. Want to stay and join us?" Lin offered Leonard a seltzer.

"Naw. I'd have to listen to too much jabbering." Leonard took a long swallow of the seltzer. "It was way too humid today. I thought I might faint earlier when I was working on the latest client's yard clearing out the brush."

Lin chuckled. "I'd like to see you faint."

"I'm serious." Leonard took a seat on one of the stools next to the island. "I can't stand the humidity. I've lost my tolerance for it."

"Must be your advanced age," Lin teased.

"What's *your* excuse then? I heard you complaining about it the other day."

Lin winked. "You must have heard wrong." She untied the string that was wrapped around the box. "Have you looked at the articles in here?"

"Only to check the dates and make sure they had some stories about the watch-dog groups." Leonard drained his can. "I didn't read them, just scanned them."

"Any mention of Marguerite's ancestor, Minister Mullins?"

"I'm sure that story is in the pile." Leonard went to the fridge for another drink.

Lin lifted the lid and gently removed some of the yellowed newspapers. "Marguerite must have loved island history since she kept all of these articles."

"That's only one box of the stuff she kept." Leonard sat down next to Lin. "I think partly she loved the history and partly she was too guilty to throw out the things that were so carefully handed down to her." Leonard popped his can open. "The attic is like an old museum. Now *I'd* feel guilty tossing anything she kept."

Lin looked at her friend with soft eyes. Leonard could seem gruff and off-putting, but in reality, he was a kind and gentle man with a heart of gold. When her grandfather died and left her the Nantucket cottage, Lin boxed most of his things and put them in storage, and like Leonard with his wife's belongings, she just couldn't part with any of her grandfather's possessions.

"Want to look through this one?" Lin carefully slid one of the old newspapers across the island to Leonard and then began to read over the one on the counter in front of her. "It seems that most of the island population didn't get involved one way or the other when Prohibition took effect."

"Most people bought what they wanted quietly and minded their own business." Leonard turned a page. "As long as groups ran their "businesses" peacefully, folks didn't want to get involved." Leonard made air quotations with his fingers when he said the word 'businesses.'

"That's understandable." Lin nodded. "It did seem to divide some of the islanders, though. Police and authorities tried to uphold the law and religious individuals spoke out against the illegal activity. The citizens who formed the watch-dog groups must have had similar reasons for getting involved."

After an hour of poring over the newspapers without finding what she wanted, Lin leaned back and stretched. "Viv will be here soon. Stay and eat dinner with us."

"I'm meeting a friend in town later." Leonard closed the paper he was reading and pushed it to the side. "Besides, if I stay, you'll make me read these articles all night long."

Lin smiled and stood to check on the pie in the oven. As she got up from her stool, her elbow caught one of the papers and it fluttered to the floor. Picking it up, Lin spotted something at the bottom of the page and her eyes went wide with excitement. "Look at this." She placed the newspaper on the island counter between her and Leonard. "Look here." Lin put her finger on one of the black ink sentences in the article.

Leonard squinted at the small type. "William Weston? Who's he?"

In her delight at finding her ghost's name in the story, she'd momentarily forgotten that Leonard didn't know about the ghost. "He was active in the citizens' groups. I saw a picture of him in one of Anton's history books."

"What's it say about him?"

Lin read quickly, eager to find any tidbit of information about the man. "Oh, listen to this." She looked up. "William Weston had a different reason for going after the smugglers. His daughter had fallen in love with a member of a smuggling ring and she ran off with him."

Leonard grunted. "The ole' man probably had someone better in mind for his daughter than a randy, bad boy smuggler. I guess that was reason enough to join the cause."

"The article says that some young women were intrigued by the adventure of the smuggling gangs ... much to the dismay of their parents."

"No doubt about that." Leonard chuckled.

"William Weston told the interviewer that he wanted to find his daughter and curtail the illegal activity around the island." Something picked at Lin's skin when she read the words.

"Time for me to head out." Leonard leaned over to pat Nicky who had pushed up sleepy-eyed from his blanket in the corner when he heard the man preparing to leave. "Keep the papers as long as you want, Coffin. I'll see you tomorrow bright and early."

Lin walked him to the door and as Leonard drove away in his truck, Viv bicycled around the corner. Holding the front door wide open, Lin waited with a big smile on her face as Viv locked her bike. Viv gave her cousin a hug. "I can tell you've got some news for me." She greeted the friendly dog with a pat and looked eagerly at Lin.

"I found something about William Weston in the papers that Leonard brought over." Leading Viv to the kitchen island to show her, Lin summarized what she'd learned.

"Having your daughter run off with some creep is a good reason to try and rid your town of those losers." Viv slung her backpack onto the counter and removed a container of salad. "Although, putting yourself in danger might not be the best idea. I understand that those smugglers could be vicious."

Lin took the shepherd's pie from the oven and set it to cool on a wire rack. The cousins set the deck table with dinner plates, napkins, and silverware all the while discussing the information about William Weston.

"It's a bit of news," Viv said, "but not a whole lot to help figure out what's going on."

"It's a clue though. I think it's important, too." Lin told Viv about the odd sensation she'd experienced when she discovered the article containing some quotes from her ghost.

They carried their food and drinks to the outside table, lit the candles, and settled down to enjoy the meal.

"What was William Weston's daughter's name?" Viv scooped a portion of shepherd's pie onto her plate.

"Rose."

"How old was she?"

"Twenty." Lin passed Viv the salad bowl.

"Did the old article say who your ghost's

daughter ran off with?"

"No. I wish it did. It would be another clue to go on."

Taking a sip of her wine, Viv held the glass and swirled the dark red liquid around. "Do you think your ghost's appearance has something to do with his daughter?"

Lin took in a deep breath and nodded. "I do, yes. It's a feeling I got when I read that Weston mentioned to the interviewer that his wife had passed away years ago and that Rose was all he had left." Lifting her napkin to her lips, she thought over the few things they knew. "I can't pull it together, but I think the ghost-workers that Mrs. Perkins sees, Rose Weston, and my ghost all have something to do with each other. We need more information."

Viv sprinkled her portion of salad with oil and vinegar. "What about the sensation you had when we were touring the Perkins mansion? Could that be a clue to what's happening?"

Lin stopped chewing and stared at Viv. "It must be." Placing her fork on her plate, she frowned. "How does it all tie together?"

"We need to do more research. After we eat, let's go through more of the old newspapers."

"I think we should try to find out who was smuggling liquor back then. We need to pay a visit to the historical museum to look things up." Lin started to feel hopeful. "Maybe we can actually figure this out." Her eyes narrowed. "If only I knew what the ghost wants from me."

"Maybe it will become clear soon." Viv gave the dog a small piece of chicken. "Keep digging. We'll get there."

Lin's phone buzzed with a text. After reading it, she lifted her head and smiled at her cousin. "It's Anton. He found some information having to do with William Weston. He wants to meet at the historical museum tomorrow."

"A break in the case." Viv raised her glass to toast with Lin.

Lin smiled, lifted her glass, and clinked it against Viv's.

CHAPTER 16

The next day in the late afternoon, Lin and Viv met Anton at the historical museum. Viv had a few employees covering for her and Lin had moved the last two clients of the day to the following morning. Arriving directly from her landscaping job and with no time to stop at home for a shower, Lin worried that she might be kicked out of the place for being dirty and stinky.

The cousins met outside and climbed the granite steps to the cool comfort of the museum. Anton was in his usual seat at the back of the main room sitting at the long polished wood table near the windows overlooking the small back garden. He looked up from his book as Viv and Lin approached and he gestured for them to take seats.

Getting right down to business, Anton flipped through his leather notebook to some of the pages at the front. "It took me a while to find anything of interest, but I was finally able to procure some materials that provided some good information. It's nothing definitive, but it may help point you in the right direction."

Lin folded her arms on the table and leaned in with interest. "Leonard's wife kept some old newspapers and I found a tidbit about William Weston. He had a daughter who ran off with a smuggler and right after that happened, William joined the watch-dog group who tried to help stop the rum running."

Anton's dark eyes stared at Lin. "I see. So Mr. Weston had some motivation other than a moral interest in halting the smuggling. A personal motivation can sometimes be more compelling than one based on an ethical concern alone."

"Did you find anything about Weston's daughter, by any chance? Her name was Rose." Viv looked down at Anton's copious notes. "We wondered if she ever returned home."

"No, nothing like that. My research has been on Mrs. Perkins and her family."

Lin's eyebrows shot up in surprise. She and Viv had focused on the ghost and trying to determine what he wanted. Lin mentally berated herself for ignoring Mrs. Perkins and her background.

Anton put his finger on a line of his handwritten notes trying to find his place. "Here. I've taken down some information. It's quite interesting. Mrs. Perkins's father, Rowan Richards, purchased the mansion on Fairview Street, the one that is currently being renovated, in 1926 and lived there until his death in 2001. The man was one hundred and one years old at the time of his passing."

Viv said, "Well, I guess Mrs. Perkins has good genes."

"His wife died in the 1980s. Richards had quite a life." Anton raised an eyebrow. "The man came to the United States from Scotland as a young boy. The family was poor. They had friends in New York City so the family settled there and worked as laborers. Rowan had more ambition, it seems, and moved to Nantucket when Prohibition was instituted to join in the rum running. I am assuming that the young man had a good business sense and strong leadership skills because, rumor has it, he was soon running the smuggling organization here on the island under an assumed name. The operation expanded and he was said to have taken over the smuggling ring in the northeast United States."

Looks of surprise washed over Viv's and Lin's faces.

Anton leaned across the table and lowered his voice even though there were only two other people sitting on the other side of the room. "At the height of their success, it is estimated that Rowan Richards and his gang were taking in about fifty million dollars a year."

Lin placed her palms on the table and pushed up straight. "What?"

Viv nearly tumbled out of her seat when she heard the amount of money that Mrs. Perkins's father was making back in the day. "Fifty million? Back in the 1920s? How much is that in today's dollars?" She rolled her eyes and put her hand up, palm facing Anton. "Don't even tell me. I don't want to know."

Anton went on. "Mr. Richards was rivaling the money that Al Capone and his gang were making in Chicago at the time. When Prohibition was on the way out, Capone used his contacts to continue in organized crime. Mr. Richards used his experience and contacts for developing legitimate businesses. He went to Europe to negotiate contracts for distribution and importation rights for gin, scotch, and other spirits. The man invested in real estate, the stock market, and many other businesses and he built an immense fortune and gave generously to charities. Mrs. Perkins was his only child and he gave her the import-export portion of his businesses which she developed into what it is today. When he died, most of his money went to universities, hospitals, and charities."

"I've never heard of Rowan Richards." Lin shook her head. "I would think he would be known for his rags-to-riches story and his business acumen and success, not to mention, the shady start to his career."

Anton explained. "The man protected his privacy with a passion. He kept out of the news, donated quietly, held his businesses under umbrella organizations and had the CEOs of those businesses take the publicity. During the last half of his life, he rarely left the island."

"So Richards bought that mansion on Fairview Street at the height of his rum running days?" Lin was trying to put things together.

"He did."

Lin speculated. "So those ghost-workers that Mrs. Perkins sees at night ... they could be men who worked for her father in the 1920s."

Viv nodded. "Those ghost-workers must be moving alcohol. They must be working in the gang of men who were employed by Rowan Richards during Prohibition. The ghosts must be reliving, if that's the right way to put it, one of their nights of smuggling of nearly a hundred years ago."

"Is Mrs. Perkins seeing the ghosts as some kind of a message from her father?" Lin's brow furrowed as she tried to understand the implications.

"If she is, then why does *your* ghost appear? What does *he* want?" Viv cocked her head to the side. "He was against the smuggling."

The cousins stared at Anton for clarification.

"No, no." Anton pushed his glasses up the bridge of his nose. "Don't look at me. I only find the information. *You* must interpret it."

Lin's shoulders sagged. "We could use some help here."

"Ask your ghost." Anton flipped through the pages of his notebook for anything he might not have told the girls. "By the way, have you received your invitation?"

Lin's eyes widened and her heart pounded with dread. "What invitation?"

"The invitation to Mrs. Perkins's house-warming event." Anton shuffled some books around on the table.

"I haven't been home yet." Lin's voice trembled slightly and she glanced at Viv. "I haven't picked up today's mail yet." She hoped that she'd been left off of the guest list and there would be no invitation in the mailbox, and then, worrying that there *was* an invitation, her mind whirled as she tried to think of possible reasons and excuses that she could use not to attend.

Viv put her hand on Lin's arm. "Don't worry about it. We'll all be there with you. John's office will be invited and I'll be going with him. Jeff will be there. Anton will be there."

"It might actually be an interesting event." Anton took a look at Lin. "Perhaps you can focus on trying to link all of the information together while you're there." Folding his hands on the table, he added, "Maybe those ghost-workers will make an appearance on the night of the event and we can all see them."

Lin scowled.

"I must run along." Anton gathered his things, stuffed them into his black leather briefcase, and dashed away.

Viv sighed. "You'll figure it out. Walk me back

to the bookstore, would you? I'm working the evening shift tonight, too."

Strolling along the brick walkways of Nantucket town, Viv and Lin discussed the information that Anton had discovered and shared with them.

"I didn't realize that illegal activities were so lucrative." Viv smiled. "Maybe I'll start dealing in illegal items. Maybe I'll make a fortune from it."

Lin looked at her cousin out of the corner of her eye. "I'm not sure you have the personality for it."

"Why not?" Viv pretended to be insulted by her cousin's doubt that she could be successful at smuggling.

"You'd worry too much and you'd end up getting caught because the police would pick up on your nervousness. You also aren't cold blooded and couldn't do the things that would be necessary. You're generous and kind and good to people."

Viv narrowed her eyes and joked. "Maybe I could change?"

"Maybe." Lin chuckled.

The girls walked past some of the beautiful antique mansions that lined Main Street and Lin wondered what was behind the fortunes of the people who built them and the fortunes of the people who owned them now. Could such wealth be amassed in legitimate ways or were such fortunes only possible through shady dealings or unfair business practices or by hurting others?

"I wouldn't mind being wealthy," Viv

announced. "Not one bit." Kidding, she narrowed her eyes and gave her cousin a gentle poke with her elbow. "Maybe I need to work on developing my ruthless side."

"It might help you increase your bank account," Lin joked. She couldn't imagine her cousin having a ruthless bone in her body. Suddenly, a tight sensation of dread gripped Lin's stomach and made her feel sick as the word repeatedly pounded in her head.

Ruthless. Ruthless.

CHAPTER 17

Under the dark sky, Lin hurried past her mailbox and gave it wide berth as if the thing might reach out and grab her if she wasn't paying attention. She didn't want to know if the box contained an invitation to Polly Perkins's house-warming event because then she could pretend that the fancy get-together wasn't going to happen. Unlocking the cottage's front door, Lin gave the mailbox a quick glance before bolting inside, slamming the door, and leaning back against it while taking in long, deep breaths. She knew it was foolish to behave the way she did, but Lin couldn't shake off the feeling of dread that consumed her over attending the event at Mrs. Perkins's newly-renovated mansion.

Nicky wagged his little tail and greeted his owner with sleepy eyes. Despite the late hour, Lin prepared a snack and decided to do some programming work for the mainland business where she was employed part-time. Having worked for the firm for a few years before deciding to move to Nantucket, she was pleased when they asked her

A Haunted Invitation

to continue to work for them remotely.

Setting her half sandwich and cup of tea on the desk in the spare second bedroom that she used as an office, she sat down at her laptop. The dog curled up on his doggy bed in the corner. Lin sighed watching the dog turn in three circles and settle, wishing her concerns were as care-free as the sweet brown creature's were.

After working for an hour, it was hard to keep her eyes open. She was about to power down her computer when she decided to stay up a little longer to do some internet searching on William Weston and Rowan Richards. There were several articles that mentioned Richards attending charity events on the island, a story on the wedding of his daughter, Polly, to Roger Perkins, and numerous references regarding his company holdings. Nothing appeared out of the ordinary for a man of his wealth, and in fact, it all lined up with how Anton described Richards ... reclusive and averse to publicity. Lin found it odd that not a single word could be found about the man's early life. It was as if Rowan Richards arrived in the world as a fully-formed adult working in business.

Lin turned her thoughts to William Weston and calculated that since his daughter was twenty years old when she ran off with a rum runner, then Weston was probably around forty at the time which meant he was most likely born around 1880. After keying the man's name into an internet search engine, Lin scanned the articles and stories, but none of them were about the correct William Weston.

Glancing at the time at the bottom of her computer screen, Lin regretted staying up so late and knew she'd pay for it the next day. Dragging herself up from the chair, she and the dog stumbled sleepily to the bedroom where they climbed into their beds. Lin shut off the light and rested back against her pillow, and just as she was about to doze off, a thought pulsed in her brain causing her to sit bolt upright blinking into the darkness. The idea that surfaced had her heart pounding and her stomach churning. *Did Rowan Richards kill my ghost? Did Richards kill William Weston?*

***

Lin couldn't wait for her workday to end so that she could hurry to the historical museum to look for information on William Weston. She wanted to find out when he'd died, and if possible, how he'd died. Her mind was so focused on the things she needed to learn that she didn't hear Polly Perkins approaching and when the woman called out to her, Lin startled.

"Hello." Mrs. Perkins came out the front door of the brick mansion. "I'm glad to see that the front garden is nearly finished."

Lin said, "Just a few finishing touches."

"Very good. Will the side garden be completed before my house-warming event?"

Lin assured the woman that the landscaping would all be done in plenty of time for her gathering.

"Did you receive the invitation to the event?" Mrs. Perkins had her hand on her hip. "I expect everyone to be in attendance."

Lin had forgotten to check her mailbox that morning. "I haven't received it."

Mrs. Perkins eyes darkened with disbelief.

Lin quickly explained. "I didn't get my mail yesterday. I'm sure the invitation will be there when I get home today."

As the woman was about to turn away, Lin took the opportunity to ask a question. "My cousin and I have been going through some old Nantucket newspapers. We read a bit about your father."

One of Mrs. Perkins's eyebrows raised and she took a step closer. "Did you?"

Lin nodded. "He seemed to be a very interesting man." She gestured to the house. "We read that your father bought the house when he was a young man."

"He did."

Even though she knew the answer to her next question, Lin asked anyway. "Did he come from a wealthy family?"

"He did not. My father was a self-made man." Mrs. Perkins's voice held a slightly arrogant tone.

Lin smiled. "How did he make his money?"

"Business." Mrs. Perkins's huffed seemingly annoyed that anyone would need to ask how a person amassed such a fortune.

"Real estate?"

"Some."

"Your father's business skills must have been quite impressive," Lin noted. "Is there a book written about him?"

"No. My father was a private man. He wouldn't cooperate with anyone who wanted to write a book about him and without his cooperation, there wouldn't be much of a book."

"I see." Lin suppressed a sigh, feeling stymied that she wasn't getting much information. "Too bad. I'm sure he would make an inspirational subject." Lin made eye contact with the older woman. "I understand that your father lived in this house until he died. This was your family home? You grew up here?"

"I did, but for middle and high school, I attended private school off-island." Mrs. Perkins brushed at her bangs.

"What a gorgeous house to grow up in." Lin turned her attention to the brick home. "What made you decide to move back here and leave your other house?"

Mrs. Perkins adjusted the gold bangles on her wrist. "I wanted closer proximity to town. I've lived out in 'Sconset for years. It's beautiful there, but I needed a change." The woman started away. "I have a meeting with my financial advisor. I'll see you later."

Lin watched Mrs. Perkins walk down the tree-lined sidewalk and then she returned to the work of planting a row of hydrangeas along the front of the house. Her mind was working overtime trying to determine the reason why she always felt so uneasy and uncomfortable in Mrs. Perkins's presence.

"Hi, hon." Jeff came around the corner with a beaming smile on his face. "The front looks great. Mrs. Perkins will be very pleased."

Lin wiped some soil from her fingers onto her jeans shorts and gave her boyfriend a hug. "Mrs. Perkins was just here. She certainly didn't gush over my work. Mostly she was glad I'd be finished with the landscaping by the time of her event." Lin shrugged. "I guess I should be glad that she didn't complain about anything."

Jeff chuckled. "If Mrs. Perkins doesn't say anything negative, then you should take it as a compliment."

Kurt, the project manager, walked up to the house and stopped to chat with Lin and Jeff about the progress on the Perkins mansion. "I'll be glad when this job is done. That woman has been on my case from day one." He slowly shook his head from side to side. "If I knew what a headache this would be, I would have declined the job."

"You work with clients like this all the time," Lin

said. "This job has been more stressful than usual?"

"I'm ready to make a career change after this." Kurt was only half-joking. "I'm definitely taking a week off to recuperate. I should have known this was going to be trouble the first day I came to talk to her."

Jeff raised an eyebrow. "What happened the first day?"

Kurt ran his hand over his short black hair. "It's the woman's peculiarities. Mrs. Perkins is demanding and she's a perfectionist. I work with these types of people all the time so I'm used to that. It was this woman's oddball refusals and orders that made the job so miserable."

"How do you mean?" Lin asked. "What happened on the first day?"

"We were going over what she wanted done." Kurt let out an exasperated sigh. "The kitchen renovation, the lower level updates. The electrical and the plumbing had to be updated. I told her what should be done and where it should be done. She agreed that it needed updating, but she insisted that the work be completed without damaging certain existing walls. It was nonsense. It cost far more than it needed to because we had to run pipes and wires around the place like a maze. I should have taken her refusal to allow things to be done the direct way as a sign she would be illogical and unreasonable throughout the project."

A Haunted Invitation

"Why couldn't you work through some of walls?" Lin knew that Kurt owned the best construction and renovation company on the island and that he had tons of experience. "Your workers would have made the walls better than they ever were."

"Mrs. Perkins told me that her father had an office down in the lower level and that she kept his papers and his things just the way he'd left them. She didn't want that space disturbed. I told her that we only needed to access a portion of the walls and ceilings, but she was adamant. She told me to do it her way or she'd get someone else. I explained how unnecessarily costly it would be. The woman was almost rude to me ... well actually, I *will* call her rude. She said I wasn't in her league, that my concerns were petty when compared with hers, that I was small-minded and if I wanted the project then I'd better be willing to do it her way."

"Yikes." Lin was appalled by Mrs. Perkins's treatment of Kurt. "Why bother with her? You have your choice of projects. Your reputation is like gold around here."

Kurt scowled. "I should have walked. I let my ego get in the way. Believe me, I won't let that happen again. I'll listen to my gut."

The conversation turned to upcoming projects, island news, and general chit-chat yet, all the while, Kurt's words were ringing in Lin's head.

Listen to my gut.

CHAPTER 18

After her work day was completed, Lin went home for a quick bite and a shower and then dropped Nicky off at the bookstore to stay with Viv and Queenie while she did an errand. Driving her truck along the roads to the Miacomet beach area, Lin clutched the steering wheel eager to reach her destination.

Libby had left Lin a voice message telling her that a man whose father had been a rum runner would be willing to speak with her about his dad's experiences and that she should go and meet him right after she finished her work.

Miacomet was located on the south side of the island and was a beautiful white sand beach with heavy surf and strong currents. Lin slowed to take the turnoff onto a sandy road that curved through small dunes and dark green brush and now and then she passed a few huge houses set on large lots. At the end of the narrow road, Lin pulled the truck to a stop in front of a cottage nestled between the sand and the dark green ground cover. The house's

A Haunted Invitation

shingles had weathered to a silver-gray color and red and white flowers overflowed from boxes set under each window.

When she stepped from her vehicle, an older man opened the front door and waved. "I'm Peter Van Helman." The man had a full head of white hair and kind brown eyes. "Come in." He led Lin through a living room full of comfortable white sofas and chairs accented with light blue and navy pillows to a covered deck at the back of the house where they sat in the shade looking out over the large stone patio to the sand dunes and the sea beyond.

"What a gorgeous place." Lin admired the quiet, peaceful spot and listened to sea birds calling in the distance.

Mr. Van Helman had carried in a tray with a glass pitcher of home-made lemonade, a carafe of iced tea, and a plate of cookies. "My wife and I enjoy baking and cooking. We have a nice garden at the side of the house where we grow vegetables and some fruit."

"Have you been here in Miacomet for a long time?" Lin sipped from her glass mixed with tea and lemonade.

"Forever. I built this house myself. My wife was very patient about how long it took me." Mr. Van Helman winked. "The woman is a saint. Mary is out with a friend. I hope she returns before you leave so you can meet her."

Lin and Mr. Van Helman shared information about their backgrounds and families and how much they loved Nantucket. "I bet you're happy to be back on-island," Mr. Van Helman said to Lin. "Once you've lived here, the place has a way of burrowing into your heart."

Lin nodded in agreement. "I'm very happy to be home."

"So, Libby Hartnett told me that you and your cousin have an interest in the history of the island. You've been reading lately about the Prohibition era?"

"We've been going through some old newspapers that we got from a friend. It's a fascinating time with the rum runners and the watch-dog groups on opposite sides of the issue."

"I've done some reading about the time and it's my opinion that Prohibition was a misguided idea which led to the rise in organized crime. Things would have been better off if Prohibition never happened." The man smiled. "It's always easy to judge with the benefit of hindsight."

"I agree with you." Lin nibbled a cookie. "The prohibition laws certainly contributed to a rise in crime networks."

"Libby told you my father was a rum runner?" Mr. Van Helman's eyes twinkled and he chuckled. "My father's adventures give our family the hint of a dangerous edge."

Lin smiled. "How did your father get into the

rum running?"

"My dad was a great storyteller. He loved to regale my brother and me with tales of his younger days." Mr. Van Helman's face softened thinking fondly of his father. "I'm sure there was some elaboration to it all, but even without the exaggeration, they were interesting stories nonetheless."

Pouring more lemonade into his glass, the man went on. "My dad was Dutch and came over to the States alone at the age of seventeen. He claimed to be older than he was. I wouldn't have had the guts to move across the ocean to an unknown place with no friends or family, but Dad did it. He landed in Boston, made a friend, and the two of them ended up moving here to the island. Prohibition had been in force for a few years and the boys had heard that there was a lot of money to be made in smuggling alcohol." Mr. Van Helman shook his head and gave Lin a smile. "If you'd met my father, you would never believe he would get involved in anything illegal. It must have been the foolishness of youth that made him think it was a good idea."

"Did your father actually join up with a gang?" Lin's eyes were wide with interest.

"He had interaction with a gang and it almost cost him his life." Van Helman sighed. "Lucky for me and my brother that Dad escaped with his life or we wouldn't be here."

A serious expression showed on Lin's face.

"What happened?"

"My dad and his friend didn't understand the workings of an organized crime ring. They were naïve and thought they could waltz onto the island and start up and run their own thing." Van Helman shook his head. "They couldn't do such a thing and they soon discovered that fact."

"The organized groups on the island found out about them and threatened them?"

"Indeed they did. In fact, one group did more than threaten them. My father and his friend were "recruited" to join the team. In other words, they were forced at gunpoint to work for the group after being beaten up and told they'd be killed if they didn't cooperate. The group was running a big smuggling operation and they had a huge deal coming up when they enlisted my dad and his friend. After the fact, my dad realized that they were being set up to take the fall should things go badly."

"*Did* the deal go badly?" Lin asked.

"The weather was terrible on the night of the transaction. They were attempting the deal out on the open water to elude the authorities and the weather went from bad to worse. The storm blew in with pelting rain, huge seas. My dad was an experienced boater, he could sail, he knew the sea well. I think that's the only way he survived that night. Three boats went out. Only one returned."

"The other boats sank? Were the men saved?"

A Haunted Invitation

Van Helman shook his head. "The men were lost, some due to the storm and others in the gunfight that took place during the smuggling run. Only two bodies washed up on shore the next day. My dad's skills helped one of the crewmembers get the boat back to port. The whole thing was a disaster."

Lin slowly shook her head imagining the terrible event.

"The boss of the gang was on my father's boat that night. He didn't usually go out on the deals, but this was a big one and he wanted to show his face to the guys they were meeting. My father had warned them not to attempt the deal due to the bad weather. Impressed with dad's boating skills during the ordeal, the boss tried to force him to remain in the group. Dad flatly refused."

"He did?" Lin was flabbergasted to hear that Van Helman's father stood up to the boss.

"Everyone on the run that night was nearly killed. Dad's friend was on one of the other boats, he died that night in the gunfight and his body was never found. The gang-boss threatened to kill my father if he didn't join the group as a permanent member. My father told the guy to go ahead and kill him because he wasn't joining. Dad stormed away."

Lin's jaw dropped in surprise. "Did the boss go after him?"

"He did not. Who knows why? Dad tried to get

work on the big fishing boats, but no one would hire him. Dad knew the gang-boss was behind it. It was the boss's way of trying to ruin dad or run him off the island."

"Your father stayed here? He didn't leave? What did he do for work?"

"He worked on a farm for a while, saved up his money and bought his own small boat. He became a small independent fisherman."

"Did that boss stay on the island or did he move away? Did your father ever run into that man again?"

"For the most part, the boss stayed on-island. After Prohibition, he became a legitimate businessman, tried to clean up his act, became a respectable community member and citizen." Van Helman narrowed his eyes. "He could put on a business suit and play a role, but the guy was still a monster. He threatened the guys who had worked for him to keep them quiet about the illegal activity of the past. They were not to mention his involvement. The ones who did speak of him were discredited and people said that they were lying in order to ruin the man's reputation. Those who persisted in spreading rumors about him, well, somehow they disappeared or met with accidents." Van Helman shrugged a shoulder. "Some people in the world are very powerful and are best avoided."

Lin looked out at the sand dunes and the blue ocean. Hearing about one of the rum runner's stories from a relative made the whole thing far more real to her.

"The world is better off without that man in it." Van Helman gave a wistful smile. "But I suppose there's always someone ready to step into the void and take his place."

Lin turned her head to ask Mr. Van Helman a question and she braced herself for the answer. "Can you tell me the boss's name?"

The older man nodded. "It doesn't matter anymore. He's gone now and he can't do any more damage. He used the fake name of Ronald Jones when he was running the smuggling rings, but his real name was Rowan Richards. Have you heard of him?"

Lin certainly had.

CHAPTER 19

Lin and Viv had been sitting in the back room of the historical museum reading through old records trying to find information on William Weston when the librarian suggested that they pull up online vital records information through the state's archives database which listed birth, marriage, and death records beginning with 1841. The girls were also pointed to a genealogical website that might be useful to them.

"That would be a lot easier than what we've been doing." Viv rolled her eyes. "Who knew those records could be accessed online?"

Lin keyed Weston's name, date range, and town of birth into the search window of the vital records database.

"Are you sure he was born on Nantucket?" Viv asked.

"No. I'm just hoping he was." Lin hit the enter button after guessing what the date range would be. Information filled the screen and Lin pointed the cursor to an entry and clicked. "Look."

A Haunted Invitation

Viv read out loud. "William John Weston was born in Nantucket Town, Nantucket, Massachusetts on January 5, 1880. Is that your ghost?"

A smile spread over Lin's face. "I think so. It must be him. Let's search for marriage records."

An entry for marriage records indicated that William Weston married Yvette Rose Millard in June 1905. The girls then searched for Weston's death record and found that he had passed away in Nantucket Town on September 5, 1928. Lin looked up and blinked after reading that the cause of death was listed as "accident."

"Accident?" Lin repeated what she saw written on the computer screen. "What kind of accident? That's it? No other information?"

"That would make him ...." Viv calculated in her head. "Forty-eight when he died?"

Lin nodded and tapped away at the computer keys. "I'm going to do a search on his daughter, Rose." She stared at the screen. "Here's her birth record. April 1906. It lists William and Yvette as her parents." After more tapping, Lin announced, "There are no marriage records listed for her. No death record either." Looking at her cousin, Lin scowled. "How can that be? How can there be no death record?"

Viv said, "There wouldn't be a death record listed for her if she moved out of state. She may have been married and died in a state other than Massachusetts. This database is only for

Massachusetts vital records."

"Oh, right." Lin's shoulders sank. "Let's take a look at the genealogical website."

Just as Lin logged out of the vital records database, the librarian returned to alert the cousins that the museum hours were over for the day and that they were about to lock up.

Viv checked the time on her phone and realized that they had overstayed by thirty minutes. They apologized for losing track of time, thanked the librarian for her help, and left the building. The setting sun painted the sky with violet and rose streaks and as the cousins walked through town past the stores and restaurants, Lin's phone rang.

Lin spoke to the caller. "Yes. That would be great. Yes, she's right here with me. Thanks so much. We'll see you soon." Clicking off from the call, Lin turned to Viv. "That was Mr. Van Helman. His brother has some photos from his father's early days on-island that he'd like to show us. Will you come?"

"Right now?" Viv asked.

Lin nodded.

"I wouldn't miss it."

The girls hurried to Viv's house to pick up her car and, in thirty minutes, they were at Mr. Van Helman's house in Miacomet. Two men who looked like twins stood at the front door waiting to greet the young women.

"This is my much older brother, Paul." Mr. Van

A Haunted Invitation

Helman smiled at his joke.

"I am also the much smarter brother." Paul countered his brother's joke with his own as he shook hands with Lin and Viv.

The cousins were ushered to the living room where several photos were scattered over the coffee table. They all took seats.

"We were just having a look at some of the old photographs," Peter Van Helman said. He recounted the story for Viv that he'd told Lin earlier in the day about his father and the rum runners.

"Our father was lucky that he wasn't killed." Paul slid a photo closer to the girls. "This is Dad here. He'd only been on Nantucket for about a month. This is his friend, the young man who was killed in the gunfight with the dealers.

Lin and Viv leaned forward to get a better look at the pictures.

"This is a photo of the gang-boss, Ronald Jones, his real name was Rowan Richards, who went on to become a very successful businessman." Paul eyed his brother who nodded and said, "I told the girls that Ronald was an alias. They knew who he really was."

Peter had a few notebooks next to him on the sofa that contained news stories and photographs. "Ronald Jones was a mastermind and that's for sure. After I'd heard Dad's stories about the rum running days and his brief membership with the group, I became interested in Ronald's life and followed news about him. I was fascinated with the man and how he became so successful. I hoped that one day I might write a book about him."

"My brother is an historian," Peter explained.

"Retired professor," Paul elaborated. "American history is my area of interest."

"You must know Anton Wilson then?" Viv asked.

"Oh, yes." Paul smiled. "Anton and I get together once a month for coffee. The talk somehow always turns to history."

Lin was interested to know more about Rowan Richards. "We understand that Ronald Jones, or Rowan Richards as he was known after the rum running days, was pretty reclusive and shunned attention of any sort. Have you gathered enough information on the man to fill a book?"

"He was indeed a very private man. There's quite a bit of anecdotal information about Rowan Richards when he was the boss of the rum running gang and the heavy-hand he used to keep control of his area and his crew. My dad introduced me to a few men who had been involved in the gang and they offered to tell me some things on the condition of anonymity. Allegedly, Rowan Richards maimed men, caused accidents, had men murdered to keep them in line or to keep their mouths closed or to use them as examples to the other members of the group to do their work and keep quiet. I don't have enough to write a book with Rowan solely as the subject. I would write about Prohibition on the island and would include information about some of the gang members and the bosses who ran the gangs." Paul raised an eyebrow and grinned. "I think that Rowan's background might be of interest to many people."

"Is it safe to write about Rowan Richards?" Viv asked.

Paul's expression turned sober. "That has been my concern for most of my adult life. Rowan has been dead for over a decade now and his loyal partners must all be dead as well. Rowan has a daughter, but I doubt that she runs her business using the same tactics that her father employed. It might be time to prepare a book for publication."

"What made that man such a monster?" Viv's voice was gruff. "How does someone have so little regard for other people? How does someone so easily and callously take another person's life?"

Paul shook his head. "It would probably take a team of psychologists to figure that out."

"Do you know much about his early life?" Lin questioned. "We know he came over from Scotland and lived with his parents in New York before he came to Nantucket."

"There isn't much available about his early life," Paul said. "I do know that he was arrested in New York several times for assault."

"So he had violent tendencies right from the start," Viv noted.

Peter said, "Rowan arrived on the island and

joined a fledgling group of smugglers. He became the leader almost immediately and expanded his territory from there."

Paul shared some other information. "When it was clear that Prohibition would end and with his plenty of contacts, Rowan began thinking about using his immense resources to invest in and develop legitimate businesses. He left Nantucket for a while, changed his appearance to fit the business world. When he ran the smuggling ring from the island, Rowan was skinny, had long black hair that he wore tied back in a ponytail. I think he fancied himself a pirate back then. He returned to using his real name, cut his hair short, lightened it, put on some weight, and always dressed in fine and tailored clothes. He hired the best lawyers and financial people to create a ring around him. He owned a good number of properties on the island even when he lived on the mainland. Eventually, Rowan moved back to Nantucket." Paul looked at the photos on the table and moved one over to show Lin and Viv. "This is one of the only other pictures of Rowan during the smuggling days."

"His eyes look a bit crazy," said Viv.

"Maybe that's because you know his character and the things he's done," Lin suggested.

"This is another picture of Dad." Paul placed a photograph on the table in front of the girls.

"Oh." Lin's heart started to race and she let out an exclamation of surprise when she noticed the man standing next to Paul and Peter's father in the photograph. It was her ghost. "Do you know this man? I think Viv and I have seen him in other photos of the time."

"Yes," Paul said. "My dad said the man's name was William. He didn't know a last name. The man was older than our father. Dad liked him."

Lin hoped to get some information about the ghost. "How did your father know him?"

Paul said, "He was one of the rum runners. William was part of the group who worked for Ronald Jones, later known as Rowan Richards."

Lin was so shocked to hear Paul say that William was a rum runner that she gaped at him with her mouth open and Viv had to step in. "I'm pretty sure this man was described as belonging to one of the citizen watch-dog groups who did what they could to help rid the island of the illegal smuggling."

Paul shook his head. "You must be thinking of someone else. Dad told us that William was a good guy, but *he was* a smuggler. He was on that ill-fated smuggling deal the night of the storm. William was the guy Dad worked with to get the boat safely returned to shore."

Lin was so baffled by this news that her head was spinning and she felt dizzy. "Did some members of the watch-dog groups infiltrate the gangs in order to report back to the police about who was involved and what was going on?"

Paul cocked his head. "It's possible, I suppose,

but I can't imagine the authorities would use citizens to do such things. Maybe members of the police force would do that."

"Though, we've never heard anything about that kind of thing," Peter said.

"I wonder if William was a police officer?" Viv tried to make sense of the matter.

Paul shook his head. "I don't think so. My father said that William told him that he'd worked in a store on Main Street for more than twenty years. He said he tired of it and wanted a chance at adventure and making some money."

With trembling fingers, Lin lifted the photograph and stared at the picture of her ghost. *What's going on?*

CHAPTER 20

"I can't believe that William Weston was a rum runner." Lin looked through the car's passenger side window at the dark night. "I just don't believe it."

"Well, maybe he *was* involved with the smuggling." Viv turned the steering wheel to move her car onto the side road. "Maybe he got killed in a deal. Maybe he blames Rowan Richards."

"So why did he choose to come back now? Why is he appearing now? Rowan has been dead for over ten years. What's the point? Why have those rum runners appeared behind the restaurant now? What's going on?"

The cousins drove along in silence for a few minutes each one thinking over the pieces of the puzzle that they'd discovered so far.

"We need to think." Lin adjusted in the seat to better face Viv. "Why the ghosts have appeared now is an important clue, but that isn't known to us right now so we have to think about what we *can* find out."

"Okay. That's right." Viv nodded. "What should we focus on?"

"I think we should try to find out whether or not William Weston was associated with the police force. That could be the reason that he was working with the smugglers, if that's even true. I think we need to find out how he died. That might be easier to figure out. If it was an accident, maybe there's a news account. We have the old newspapers from Leonard that we can look through."

"I'll drive to your house then and we can spend some time looking at the newspapers."

In a few minutes, Lin and Viv were curled up on the sofa with the dog asleep in between them. They read through news accounts from the past using William Weston's date of death that they'd been able to get from the online database to narrow down when an article might show up in the news about his accident. Checking papers up to two weeks after the man's death date revealed nothing and the cousins sat back on the sofa deflated.

"Now what?" Viv asked.

"William Weston must be buried on the island." Lin stretched her legs out and rested them on the ottoman. "Tomorrow I'll call the island cemeteries and ask if William is buried there."

"How will finding his grave help us figure out how he died?" Viv yawned.

Lin leveled her eyes at Viv. "Tomorrow I'm

going to make another call to someone else. I have an idea, but I'm not sure if the person I'm going to call will agree to it."

***

Lin parked her truck in the cemetery parking lot and slid out of the driver's seat. She opened the back door for the dog so that he could jump out. They walked around to the passenger side just as the woman got out and shut the vehicle door.

"Thanks for coming with me." Lin smiled at Libby Hartnett.

"The ghost is in need." Libby looked over the peaceful cemetery that had large trees ringing the area. Birds chirped and a gentle breeze cooled the air. "We have to try and help."

The cemetery worker who Lin had spoken to on the phone gave her directions to William Weston's plot and Lin led the way up the slight incline to the far corner of the cemetery. When the spot was located, the two women stood quietly looking down at the headstone and the dog sat down next to it.

"I don't do this very often anymore." Libby turned to Lin. "It's exhausting for me. It takes days for me to recover."

"Are you sure you want to do this?"

"I feel a duty." Libby closed her eyes for a moment and took in a deep breath.

"Should I tell you more about him, my ghost?"

"No. It's best to just let it happen." Libby reached out her hand to Lin. "Ready, Carolin?"

Libby Hartnett had a special skill that she'd shared once with Lin several months ago when Lin had returned to the island. The two women were distant relatives and Libby had been helping to guide Lin as she came to terms with and tried to develop her skills of seeing and helping ghosts. Libby had a different ability. Libby could sometimes see what had happened to a person almost like watching an episode of a television show. If she held the hand of someone with special skills, then that person might be able to see what Libby saw.

Lin took in a long breath and grasped the older woman's hand. The two closed their eyes and tried to empty their minds and slow their breathing and after a minute, the breaths they took became synced with one another. Lin's hand buzzed slightly as if a tiny electrical current ran between herself and Libby. Slowly, Lin experienced the sensation of entering a dream state, her muscles warmed and relaxed and it almost felt like she was floating on the air. Her vision began to dim until it went completely black and she squeezed Libby's hand for reassurance.

A pinhole showed in the center of the blackness and bit by bit the hole expanded until Lin could make out several people standing outside somewhere in the darkness. The images were not

A Haunted Invitation

fully clear ... it seemed as if she was looking through a blurry window. Slowly, the sound got louder like a volume knob was being turned up and she began to make out some words.

Three men, dressed in 1920s-style clothing, stood outside a large brick building down near the docks smoking cigarettes being careful to stay out of the light of the streetlamp. It was late at night and the streets were empty.

"What's taking so long? Where is he?" A tall, skinny man shuffled from foot to foot. "I wanna' go home." He threw the butt of his cigarette onto the cobblestones in the road.

"He'll be here. Keep your shirt on." A stocky, bald man growled and then cursed the chill in the air. "It's September already. Bah."

Footsteps could be heard in the distance coming down the brick sidewalk towards the men.

"This better be him." A scruffy, young guy tossed his cigarette away and rolled up his sleeves.

William Weston stepped into the pooled light from the streetlamp and stopped short when he saw the three men standing in the shadows. Worry and alarm washed over his face and he took a step back. This was not who he had expected to meet here on the dark corner.

Lin's heart pounded like a drum as she watched what was happening.

"Hey there, Will." The tall, skinny man spoke and moved closer to Weston who shuffled back one more step.

"Evening," Weston managed as he attempted to move past the men blocking his path.

"Not so fast." The younger guy grabbed Weston's arm.

"What do you want?" Weston struggled to wrench his arm from the man's grasp but without success.

"It's not what we want, you know," the bald guy told him. "You're a good guy, Will. It's what the boss wants."

Even in the darkness, it was obvious that Weston's face had paled. He glanced up to the top floor windows of the brick building. "Why? I've been doing my job."

"It's not for us to decide." The bald man lurched forward and punched Weston in the stomach.

Lin tried to cry out, but her voice was silent.

The other two men were on Weston in a split second and, in no time flat, the man lay sprawled on the sidewalk facedown, unconscious.

"Get him up." The bald man glanced around to be sure no one had witnessed the assault. "Carry him."

The other two men pulled Weston up and draped his arms over their shoulders like the man was drunk and had passed out and they were bringing him home.

"Let's go, into the water with him." The bald man started off to lead the way down the empty streets to the waterfront and as he went, he looked up briefly to the top floor of the brick building and nodded. "Let's get this over with," he muttered to his accomplices.

They hauled the unconscious man away down the street with his feet limp and bumping along the cobblestones. As they disappeared around the corner of a storefront, slight movement could be seen in the window of the top floor of the building that stood next to the walkway where the attack on Weston was carried out. A man watched for a few seconds from the window until the three men and Weston were out of sight. Turning away, the moonlight shined on the man's long dark hair held back in a ponytail.

Rowan Richards.

***

Lin coughed and startled from the vision, finding herself sitting on the grass in front of William Weston's gravestone. Her heart was still pounding and beads of sweat covered her forehead. Nicky had his front paws on Lin's lap and was licking her face. Lin turned to find Libby and saw her leaning forward with one hand holding on to the top of the headstone while her other hand pressed against her eyes.

Lin gave the dog a pat, scrambled up, and darted to Libby. She placed a hand gently on the older woman's shoulder. "Are you okay?"

Libby lifted her head, her face was ashen. "I'm okay." Her voice was barely audible. "I just need to rest." Lin helped lower her to the grass and sat down next to her.

"My ghost, William Weston, was murdered." Lin's breathing was shallow and quick. "Those men beat him unconscious and threw him into the ocean. He must have drowned." A full minute passed. "The man in the building with the ponytail. Did you see him in the vision?"

Libby nodded. She looked stricken and weak. "Who was he?"

"He was the boss of a smuggling gang during Prohibition. At the time, he went by the name of Ronald Jones. He was a monster." Lin told Libby the terrible things she'd learned about the man.

"What happened to him? That boss."

"He became a very wealthy man. He tried to hide his past in order to become a respectable business owner. His daughter lives on-island."

Libby faced Lin with narrowed eyes. "Who is his daughter?"

"The man's real name was Rowan Richards. His daughter is Polly Perkins."

Libby's eyes went wide and she shook her head. "I wonder if that woman knows about her father and his crimes."

Nicky squeezed between Lin and Libby and leaned against the older woman. Libby ran her hand over the dog's fur. "Was this experience helpful to you, Carolin?"

"It was." Lin hugged Libby. "Thank you for helping me. Now I know what happened to William."

Lin looked across the wide space of the cemetery. *Now I need to figure out why.*

CHAPTER 21

Lin was completing the landscaping work on Mrs. Perkins's side yard by planting hydrangeas, hostas, day lilies, and several other different perennials. The small side garden was surrounded by a high cedar fence and had a brick walkway that curved in the grass and led to a large cedar and wrought iron gate that opened to the expansive rear yard. The gate had been locked the entire time Lin had worked the job at Mrs. Perkins's mansion.

All the while that she dug holes, mixed in some fertilizer and peat moss, and placed the plants into the prepared spots in the ground, ideas about William Weston and Rowan Richards swirled in Lin's mind. Did William manage to join the group of smugglers in order to weaken or sabotage their organization? Did Rowan discover William's purpose and order his murder?

Lin did not believe that William joined the illegal group to make money and find adventure. He had been a member of the citizens' watch-dog group prior to joining the smugglers so Lin speculated that William must have felt that the citizens' group was ineffective and decided to do something drastic by joining the smugglers to try to bring them down by working from within.

Lin tamped the soil around the base of the hosta she'd just planted and stood up. Nicky rested on the grass watching his owner's progress on the garden. "I think that's why William joined the smugglers, Nick. It's the only thing that makes any sense."

The little dog jumped to his feet and let out a woof of agreement.

Lin heard the creak of a hinge and, surprised, her eyes flicked to the large cedar gate as it opened. Kurt came into the side yard with a concerned expression on his face.

"Oh, hi." Kurt seemed distracted and in a hurry. His mouth turned down and his forehead was creased with worry as he rushed along the brick walk to the front of the building.

"You okay?" Lin looked at him with concern.

"My daughter's camp called just now." Kurt kept walking. "My daughter has a terrible headache and feels sick. I'm going to pick her up."

"I hope she feels better soon," Lin called after him. Watching Kurt hurry away to help and comfort his little girl, something pinged in her head. "That must be it."

Lin removed her gardening gloves and pushed a stray strand of her hair behind her ear as she considered her ghost's motivations. "William's daughter ran off with a smuggler." Looking down at her dog, Lin sighed. "Did you see how worried Kurt was about his daughter? My bet is that William probably wasn't really concerned about the illegal alcohol. He was worried about his daughter and wanted her to be safe."

Nicky wagged his tail.

"We have some research to do after work tonight." Lin returned to the landscaping hopeful that she was on the right track.

After two more hours of planting and mulching, Lin opened her cooler and removed her sandwich, a large bottle of water, and a bowl for Nicky. She looked around for the dog. "Time for lunch, Nick. Come here, boy."

Lin's smile faded. The little brown creature was nowhere to be seen. Lin hurried to the front gate and pushed against it to check if it had stayed open since Kurt exited the property that way. The gate was latched. For a moment, Lin stood dismayed and then she realized that the back gate might not have latched properly when Kurt came through it to the side yard on his way to pick up his daughter.

Lin rushed to the back gate worried that the dog was in the yard at the rear of the property and she hoped that Mrs. Perkins was not at home so that Nicky would not incur her wrath as he frolicked on the property's lush lawns. Pushing through the gate, Lin's head turned from side to side scanning

A Haunted Invitation

the sweeping rear grass and gardens for her dog. Groaning, Lin started for the back of the space thinking that Nicky might be having fun stalking some chipmunks or birds or squirrels.

She wasn't worried that he'd dig or damage or disturb anything as she'd trained him not to do such things, but she knew Mrs. Perkins would have a fit that a dog was loose in her garden just a few days before her event was to take place. Lin sped around trees and checked under bushes and plantings, all the while calling the creature's name. Unable to find the dog, she started back to the side yard, her heart pounding, worried that Nicky had run off or worse, that someone had taken him.

On the mansion's lower level, wide glass doors were open and a tall man who Lin recognized as part of Kurt's crew stood on the stone patio looking around. When he spotted Lin, he waved her over. "That little brown dog is yours, right?"

Lin nodded and glanced behind the man. "Have you seen him?"

"He raced by me while I was laying tiles in the wine room." The tall man led Lin into the lower level. "I followed for a few seconds, but I lost him. I thought you'd have better luck than me getting him out of the house so I came to find you."

Lin thanked the man as they moved through the lower level's rooms. Her emotions swung from relief that Nicky had been found to annoyance that the dog had done such an uncharacteristically foolish thing. "He never behaves like this."

Lin couldn't help but admire the beauty of the rooms they were walking through. Dark, polished wood lined the walls of a wine tasting room and light sparkled through the glass of four stained-glass windows on the far wall. A circular wooden table and six high-backed chairs sat in the middle of the space on a beautiful antique area rug.

"Did you see which way he went?" Lin asked as they left the wine tasting room and entered a multi-level media room furnished with brown leather sofas and chairs which faced a large screen hanging on one of the walls.

"I thought he headed this way." The tall man checked around the room.

Lin called for the dog.

"Just don't call too loudly." The man warned Lin. "Mrs. Perkins is due back any minute."

Anxiety flooded Lin's body. She wanted to find Nicky and get out of the house. "Where could he be?"

A long hallway led away from the rooms they were in and Lin started in that direction.

"We don't go down there," the tall man said.

About to turn away, Lin was engulfed in a shaft of freezing air and she slowly shifted her eyes to the hallway. A gasp of surprise caught in her throat when she saw the cause of the cold. Her ancestor, Sebastian Coffin, stood outside an open door off of the hallway. Sebastian held Lin's eyes for a moment and then his translucent atoms began to sparkle until they flared out and he was gone.

Lin hurried down the hallway.

The worker called to her. "Wait a second. We aren't supposed to go that way."

Lin ignored the man and headed to the door which opened into a luxurious bedroom. The worker reluctantly followed. When Lin stepped inside, she stopped short as her head spun and her vision dimmed for a moment. As she sucked in deep breaths trying to control the sense of vertigo, the man didn't notice her distress and he knelt to search under the king-sized bed. "Not under here."

Lin closed her eyes for a moment and balled her hands into fists fighting the strange feeling of alarm that had overcome her. Opening her eyes, she whirled around and stormed towards a door on the side wall of the bedroom.

The door was open a few inches. Her body feeling weak, Lin gripped the doorknob, steeled herself, and flung the door wide.

Nicky sat against the back wall of the enormous, empty walk-in closet. He pointed his nose to the ceiling and let out a deep, low whine that sent chills down Lin's back. She rushed forward and scooped the dog into her arms.

"Let's get out of here." The tall workman hurried out of the bedroom without waiting to see if Lin was following.

Holding the whining animal, Lin was desperate

to leave the mansion and get outside and she was right on the man's heels as they practically jogged through the rooms. "What's wrong with you, Nick? Shush now."

As soon they reached the patio, Lin's agitation eased a bit. Thanking the man for his help, she promised to check the gate so that the dog would not be able to escape again. When she got to the side yard, Lin placed the dog on the grass. "What was that about, Nick?"

Her leg muscles shaky and weak, Lin sank down on the grass. Nicky crawled onto her lap and settled there acting shy and shook up. He looked up at Lin's face and whined again. Lin didn't know why, but she felt like crying. She wrapped her arms around the dog and rested her head against his.

Jeff opened the front gate and stepped into the side yard. "Lin? You here?" When he spotted his girlfriend and Nicky sitting together on the grass, Jeff hurried over to them and knelt, putting his arm around Lin's shoulders and running his hand down Nicky's back. "What's happened? What's wrong?"

Lin lifted her face and leaned into Jeff. She told him what had happened and how she'd felt inside the house. "Nicky is upset, too."

Jeff looked from Lin to the dog and the tension and anxiety coming off of them was almost tangible. Pulling Lin closer, he glanced up at the brick mansion. "Don't go in there without me. No matter what. Don't go into that house alone."

A Haunted Invitation

Lin raised her hand to touch her horseshoe necklace and she looked up at her boyfriend. "Sebastian Coffin was in there."

Worry pulled Jeff's facial muscles down. He tightened his grip on Lin's hand.

"Something terrible happened in there." A tear escaped from Lin's eye and traveled down her cheek. "I can feel it."

Jeff's strong hand brushed away the tiny drop of water from Lin's skin. Pressing her cheek into Jeff's palm, Lin said, "And I have to find out what it was."

CHAPTER 22

Lin stood at the beverage counter of Viv's bookstore talking things over with her cousin while Nicky and Queenie rested side-by-side in the upholstered chair next to a display table of new books. "I was so thankful that Jeff was there. He made me feel much better."

"What's up with that house?" Viv's lower lip trembled. "What was Rowan Richards doing in there?"

A petite older woman with short black hair paid for her large vanilla latte and glanced at Viv with a scowl. "Nothing good, I can tell you that."

Lin and Viv turned to the woman with wide eyes.

"Why do you say that, Paulina?" Viv addressed the customer who came in every late afternoon, rain or shine, for her vanilla latte. "Did you know Rowan Richards?"

"I knew him alright." The woman's brown eyes darkened. "I'm not a suspicious person... well, maybe I am, but what I heard in that house made my skin crawl."

A Haunted Invitation

Lin stared at the short, stocky woman wondering how she knew Rowan Richards. "I'm Lin, Viv's cousin."

"Oh, I'm sorry." Viv was so surprised by Paulina's comments that she'd forgotten to introduce her to Lin. "This is Paulina. She comes in every day."

"How did you know Rowan?" Lin's heart thudded hoping to hear something about the businessman.

"I work as a PCA, a personal care attendant." Paulina lifted her drink to her lips and sipped. "It's not for everyone, but I like the work. I like to help people. I got hired to care for Mr. Richards. I worked with him for about three years." The woman shook her head. "I quit the year before he died. He must be dead now, what? Over ten years?"

Viv suggested that they sit at one of the café tables and the three of them moved to a table in the corner.

"Why did you quit?" Viv leaned forward to hear what Paulina had to say.

"At first, Mr. Richards was quiet and easy to work with. As time went on, his mind wasn't so great. He could be nasty, contrary, uncooperative. I don't mind that. I work with lots of people who become difficult as they age."

"What was different with Mr. Richards that made you decide to give your notice?" Lin was impatient to hear about Paulina's experience with the man.

Paulina's lips were held tight together in a thin line. "Like I said, I'm not suspicious, but, well, I didn't like the things Richards was saying. It made me very uncomfortable."

Lin's heart jumped into her throat. Did Rowan Richards confess his evil deeds to Paulina? "What did he say to you?"

Paulina shifted nervously in her seat. "He started to act odd, often in the evening. He said...." The dark-haired woman looked over her shoulder and then she lowered her voice. "He told me duppies came to him."

Confusion furrowed Viv's brow. "Duppies?"

Lin made eye contact with her cousin. "Duppies are ghosts."

Viv's mouth dropped open. "Ghosts?"

"My momma was Jamaican," Paulina said. "She believed in such things. I don't, really, but the way Mr. Richards talked about them, I didn't want to stay there anymore. I didn't want to work there anymore."

"What did he say?" Viv looked horrified. "He saw ghosts?"

"That's what he said." Paulina nodded with authority. "He told me the duppies were angry. He called them ghosts. He said they came at night. Lots of them. They haunted him over the things he'd done."

A Haunted Invitation

"Did he say what he'd done wrong?" Lin stared at Paulina.

Paulina shook her head. "He never mentioned what he'd done. And I sure didn't ask him what he'd done. No way I was listening to that. Mr. Richards would get agitated and fearful when darkness came." The woman harrumphed. "He was a hundred years old when I quit the job. He knew he wasn't long for this world. Most people would get agitated when they're looking down into the jaws of hell. I say, you should have been concerned about how you lived your life a long time before now."

"So you quit?" Viv asked.

"I did." Paulina held tight to her cup. "I didn't want those duppies haunting me. What if they got confused about who needed to be haunted? I was in that house with Mr. Richards most days and well into the evenings. I got scared when he was carrying on about ghosts and spirits. I was afraid I'd see one. I didn't need that." Paulina looked from Viv to Lin. "You wouldn't want to see one, either, I imagine."

Lin didn't respond.

Paulina continued. "I know ghosts aren't real. But the way that man carried on, it made me nervous. It gave me a chill."

At the word "chill," Lin eyed her cousin thinking that if Paulina had felt a chill then there must have been ghosts visiting Rowan Richards. "You made the right decision. No one should be uncomfortable in their work." Lin nodded reassuringly. "Did Mr. Richards's daughter hire you for the job?"

Paulina's eyes narrowed and she gave a slight nod of her head. "Yes, Mrs. Perkins, she hired me."

"What did you think of Mrs. Perkins?" Viv pushed her bangs away from her eyes.

"Not much." Paulina took a swallow of her latte. "She seemed kind of bossy and superior, almost rude. I didn't have much to do with her. She didn't visit her father much. The nurse was the one in charge of the care."

"Did Mr. Richards talk to the nurse about the ghosts?" Lin questioned.

"He didn't. I was the one who did the daily activities and care. The nurse was there to supervise everything and handle the medications. When Mr. Richards would whisper to me about the ghosts, he always made sure no one else was around to hear." Paulina finished her coffee. "I need to get to my next job." As she gathered her things to go, she said, "Mr. Richards must have done a whole heap of bad during his life. In all my years, I never heard anyone mention so many duppies." Paulina wished the cousins a good evening and headed out of the bookstore.

"A whole heap of bad," Viv repeated.

"Ain't that the truth." Lin sighed. "And I'm sure that some part of that heap of bad happened right there inside Rowan Richards's house."

A Haunted Invitation

The girls discussed the case ... what they knew and what they didn't know. Lin told Viv again about that day's experience at the mansion with Nicky, and when she finished the story, her body gave an involuntary shiver. "Nicky knows there's something wrong in that house. He feels it, too."

Viv's forehead scrunched up in thought. "You told me about Kurt going off to pick up his daughter today because she was feeling sick. You said it made you think again about William Weston and the concern he must have had over his daughter, Rose, running off with one of the smugglers. I think you're right about Weston joining the smugglers to get some information about Rose." Viv stood up. "Let's go use my office computer."

A look of surprise showed on Lin's face as she got up to follow her cousin. Nicky and Queenie jumped down from the chair and trotted after the two young women.

Viv sat at her desk tapping at the keyboard.

"What are you looking up?" Lin sat in the chair next to the desk.

"Rose Weston. Let's search marriage records in the Massachusetts database. Maybe we can find out if she ever married the guy she ran off with and where she ended up. You told me her middle name was Yvette, right?"

Lin nodded and leaned over her cousin's shoulder peering at the desktop computer screen.

Viv let out a sigh. "Huh. Nothing in

Massachusetts."

Queenie growled low in her throat and gave Viv's arm a nudge.

"Try Connecticut or New Hampshire." Lin thought that Rose and her smuggler might have wanted to stay near the seacoast.

"Nothing." Viv sat back. "Maybe Rose never married. Maybe she escaped being married to the loser."

Nicky let out a woof that made both girls jump. Something pinged in Lin's chest. She swallowed hard. "Try New York."

Viv tapped away and clicked on an entry that came up. "Oh, God."

Lin stood to get a closer look at the screen and when she saw it, her heart sank and she slumped into her seat. "Oh, no."

"Ronald Jones." Viv's voice was soft. "Rose Weston married Ronald Jones." Turning to Lin with concerned eyes, Viv used the smuggler's real name. "Rose married Rowan Richards."

CHAPTER 23

Lin and Jeff and Viv and John walked along the brick walkways of a side street in Nantucket town on the way to Polly Perkins's house-warming event at her renovated brick mansion on Fairview Street. The men were dressed in light-weight, fitted summer suits. Viv wore sandals and an ankle-length soft yellow and white dress accented with silver and gold drop earrings. Lin had her hair up in a high ponytail and she had on a pale blue sleeveless summer dress that flared slightly at the knees. Silver hoop earrings and her horseshoe necklace hanging delicately around her neck on a long white gold chain completed her outfit.

The sun was low in the sky and some of the old-fashioned streetlamps had begun to flicker on as the two couples passed by nicely-tended homes and mansions in the historic district of town. Red, white, and pink roses climbed trellises and spilled over white fences. Flower boxes and planters overflowed with impatiens, geraniums, and petunias. Passing by the homes, Lin could see some people sitting on their front porches chatting with one another and small gatherings of families and friends sitting around wooden tables on stone patios in their side yards enjoying dinners and drinks.

Lin loved this time of day when lights glimmered on, the air cooled, the clink of silverware on plates could be heard through open windows, and the scent of the ocean drifted by on the light summer breeze. None of those things could calm or warm her heart in the usual way as she walked along with her boyfriend, cousin, and close friend. Lin's muscles were tense and adrenaline pulsed through her veins making her stomach feel tight and empty and she wished she was home in her cozy living room working on a crossword puzzle while Jeff sat next to her reading and the dog snoozed on his bed in the corner. Most of all, she wished she'd declined the invitation to Mrs. Perkins's event.

Rounding the corner, they could hear a band playing, the chatter of a large group, and the occasional burst of laughter punctuate the air. Several police officers stood near the curb in front of the mansion monitoring the cars arriving and the valets driving vehicles away, and they helped to direct party-goers through the gate at the side yard to the large white tents set up on the manicured lawns at the back of the property.

"Well, well." Viv watched the parade of finely-dressed men and women emerge from expensive automobiles and parade along the walkway to the rear of the mansion. "I feel like we're at the Oscars or something."

"No red carpet?" John joked.

A flutter of nervousness ran over Lin's skin and she glanced down the road to the small lot behind the restaurant of the Founders Inn.

"Shall we?" Jeff took Lin's hand, and aware of her unease about attending the event, he held it tightly as the four young people joined the small groups of guests walking to the back gardens of Polly Perkins's mansion.

The back lawns looked beautiful with the two large white tents set up on either side of the brick walk that led to the rear gardens, the pergola, gazebo, and koi pond. The band was set up in one corner of a tent and a wooden dance floor had been set in front of it.

Tables groaned with food, drink, and desserts spread out like a Roman banquet. Vases and baskets of fresh flowers had been placed on tables and columned-stands and the floral scent danced on the warm air. Gas torches stood blazing at the periphery of the property and at the side of the walkways. Strings of tiny, white lights had been laced along the ceilings of the tents where they sparkled like stars over the groups of party-goers.

The music's happy notes and the beauty of the surroundings eased Lin's tension and she felt herself begin to relax. Friends and associates spotted the foursome and came over to join them.

Kurt and his wife stood with the group. "I hate these things." Kurt ran his index finger along his starched white collar tugging it away from his neck.

Kurt's wife chuckled and winked at Lin and Viv. "Kurt doesn't do well in dress-up clothes."

"How's your daughter feeling?" Lin asked.

"She's much better. Still not a hundred percent, but she's getting there." Kurt nodded and thanked Lin for asking.

Kurt's wife smiled. "Grandma's with her tonight."

After a few more minutes of conversation, Lin and Viv wandered away to the drinks table.

Right after discovering that Rose Weston had married Rowan Richards, Viv and Lin stayed in Viv's bookstore office to search the state databases for Rose's death certificate to find out when and where she had died.

"My ghost must have joined the smugglers to try and find his daughter. I bet William Weston had no idea that Rose had taken up with the smuggling boss himself."

Viv had nodded in agreement. "And I'd bet money that Rowan Richards found out who William was and what he was after and had him killed to keep him from interfering with his relationship with Rose."

Tapping away on her keyboard, Viv had searched death certificates in every New England state, in

New York and New Jersey, and in every other state that lined the Eastern seaboard looking for information on Rose with no success. Disheartened and discouraged, the two gave up for the night and headed home.

"Tonight is the last time we'll be able to get into the mansion." Lin looked over her shoulder at the groups of people who had gathered at the lower level glass doors for the next tour of the renovated house. "If we don't figure things out tonight, it's going to be very difficult to ever find out what happened in that house."

Viv picked up a glass of champagne from the white-cloth covered table. "Most people will go on the tour early in the evening. Let's keep an eye on the door and wait until the throngs thin out. Then we'll go inside."

"Later on, people will have had a few drinks and there will be less chance of anyone paying attention to us." Lin requested a glass of sparkling water with lemon. "I have to keep my wits about me," she explained her drink choice to her cousin.

When Viv wandered off to locate the restrooms that had been set up outside, Lin stood near the corner of the mansion watching the festivities while she waited for Viv to return. With a look of alarm and annoyance on her face, Polly Perkins tore around the side of her brick home wearing a long, flowing lavender, ankle-length dress. Rushing past Lin, she noticed the young woman and stopped.

"Those workers are back." Mrs. Perkins fussed, her eyes flashing.

"Who?" Lin asked.

"Those men." Mrs. Perkins's hands were clenched into fists and Lin instinctively took a step back away from the angry woman. "Those men who work late at night behind the restaurant, they're at it again. It's an outrage. No one will stop them. I saw them from the upstairs window. They're making such a racket. They'll ruin my get-together."

Lin could see tiny beads of sweat forming on Mrs. Perkins's upper lip. "I can't hear them back here. I don't think their noise will disturb your guests."

"*I* can hear them." The older woman practically shouted the words.

"Why don't you ask the police officers out front to go by the lot and tell the men to stop the noise?" Lin knew full well that the police officers wouldn't be able to see the ghost-men working, but she thought she needed to offer a suggestion since Mrs. Perkins looked like she was about to have a public meltdown.

Flames shot from the woman's eyes. "I did that already. They told me no one was back there. As usual."

Lin thought of something and her heart thudded double-time. "Do you want to show me what you see back there? Can you see the men from inside the house? Maybe I could go over and ask them politely to stop for a few hours. Shall we go inside and you can show me?"

Some tension drained from Mrs. Perkins's face as she considered Lin's proposal. "Come with me." She whirled and strode away to the lower-level doors.

Lin looked over her shoulder to see if Viv was heading back, but didn't see her among the crowd. Not wanting to miss the opportunity to get inside the mansion, Lin hurried after Mrs. Perkins who stopped briefly at the doors and said something to the tall young man whose job it was to keep guests out of the mansion unless they'd gathered for one of the tours. The man glanced at Lin who was coming up behind Mrs. Perkins and he gave the older woman a nod. Polly Perkins gestured for Lin to follow and when they stepped into the large, luxuriously furnished sitting room and headed for the small elevator in the hall, a wave of cold air swirled around Lin with such force that she nearly gasped and choked.

Standing like sentries, one on each side of the elevator doors, were the shimmering forms of William Weston and Sebastian Coffin.

CHAPTER 24

Shaking, Lin stepped into the elevator with Mrs. Perkins.

"What's wrong with you?" Mrs. Perkins noticed the young woman's odd and shivering demeanor.

"The air conditioning chilled me and I don't like elevators," Lin fibbed. Her throat was tight and her head was spinning. *William and Sebastian together. They didn't indicate that I shouldn't go with Mrs. Perkins so I mustn't be in danger.* Lin tried to calm herself by breathing slowly and deeply. She looked out of the corner of her eye at Mrs. Perkins. *I have to figure this out.*

The elevator doors opened to the second floor and Lin followed the mansion's owner down a long hallway and into a huge bedroom with a king-sized bed placed against one wall. On the opposite side of the room, two easy chairs covered in white fabric stood before a fireplace with a marble surround and a polished wood mantle. An oil painting of sailing ships at sea hung on the wall above the mantle.

"Here." Mrs. Perkins swung open a long wide

window and pointed. "There they are. There are more of them than usual." The woman scowled and her voice dripped with annoyance. "How are the police unable to find them?"

Lin leaned close to the open window and craned her neck to see down the street and into the small lot behind the inn. The space was empty. Straightening up, Lin looked Mrs. Perkins in the eyes. She wanted to declare that there were no men working in the lot, there was no noise, and that only Mrs. Perkins could see and hear the men because they were ghosts, but now wasn't the time. "Have they been working every night?"

"Yes. Every night this week. I can't get any sleep." Mrs. Perkins rubbed her temple. "It's driving me insane."

"I'll go talk to them." Lin gave the woman a gentle smile. "They might listen to me. Will you take me back downstairs? My friends will be looking for me. I'll tell them I'm going over to the inn for a minute and that I'll be right back."

A look of gratitude showed in the older woman's eyes. "Yes. See what you can do. Please."

They returned to the elevator and descended to the lower level. As they walked through the sitting area to the glass doors, Lin spoke. "Is there a rest room down here that I can use?"

Mrs. Perkins started back to the hall to show Lin where the room was.

"Just give me directions. I don't want to keep

you from your guests. I'll go right down to the inn as soon as I use the bathroom."

Mrs. Perkins told Lin where to go and then turned for the door and exited out to the party.

Lin breathed a sigh of relief. As she turned for the hall, she nodded and smiled at the young guard who was standing by the doors watching her. Out in the hallway, she'd hoped that William and Sebastian would be waiting for her, but the space was empty. Moving down the corridor away from the sitting room, Lin tried to slow her breathing and clear her mind. She needed to get to that bedroom where Nicky had been hiding in the walk-in closet. She'd nearly passed out in that room the other day. Lin knew that whatever terrible thing had happened in the house, it had taken place near that room.

Reaching the bedroom at the end of the hall, Lin stood outside the closed door afraid to open it. Once inside, she had no idea what she would do ... she only knew that the answer to her questions were there in that room. Slowly she turned the knob and stepped in.

The room was dark and Lin fumbled for a switch. When her hand hit it, she flicked the button and the bedroom flooded with light. Lin let out a long, relieved breath when she saw the space was empty and she began to shuffle around trying to pick up on anything.

A gust of freezing air engulfed her and made her

teeth chatter. Her eyes darted around, expecting William or Sebastian to be visible, but she was alone. Reaching up, she ran her finger over her horseshoe necklace and tried to slow her racing heart. Stepping around the space, she could feel the coldest air at the back of the room so she placed her palm against the smooth cream-colored wall and for several minutes, moved her hand inch by inch over it. Little sparks began to bite into Lin's hand as if an electric current was running through the wall.

Suddenly sensing someone in the room behind her, Lin yanked her hand off of the wall and whirled around to see Polly Perkins standing just inside the doorway watching her with cold eyes. The look of hate on Mrs. Perkins's face nearly knocked Lin over.

"I waited for you outside." The woman's voice was hard. "I decided I'd go over to the lot with you. When you didn't come back out, I thought maybe you couldn't find the bathroom so I came in to look for you. The bathroom was empty."

Lin swallowed. She started to make up something about why she'd wandered into the bedroom, but abandoned the idea and decided to confront the woman. "Why didn't you let the plumbers run the pipes where Kurt wanted to place them during the renovation?"

Mrs. Perkins's eyes went wide, surprised by Lin's question.

"You didn't want them to disturb your father's den, right? You didn't' want his things disturbed. That was the reason you gave the contractors." Lin paused for a moment. "That's a lie though, isn't it?"

Mrs. Perkins's facial muscles tightened and she took a step forward. "What are you talking about?" Her nostrils flared as she sucked in quick breaths.

"Your father did something in this house. Here on this level, right behind this wall." Lin pointed. "He walled up the space, didn't he? To hide what he'd done. That's the reason the plumbers couldn't go through there." Lin's head was pounding so hard that it felt like it was about to explode. "What's in there?"

"Get out of this room. You aren't supposed to be in here." Mrs. Perkins's face was as red as a beet and her arms were flailing about. "You're trespassing. Get out," she shrieked.

Lin lowered her voice. "You're the only one who can see the workers behind the inn's restaurant."

Mrs. Perkins looked like she'd been struck. "What?"

"No one else can see those workers, only you can see them. That's because those men are ghosts."

Mrs. Perkins's hand flew to her chest and she gasped. She tried to blink back the tears that threatened to overflow, but there was no stopping them and they tumbled out of the woman's eyes and spilled down her cheeks. "No, no."

"Yes." Lin nodded and moved two steps closer.

A Haunted Invitation

"The ghosts come every night because of what your father did. They won't stop showing up until you make it right."

"No." Mrs. Perkins's eyes were glassy. She held up her hand and backed out of the room.

"You need to make it right," Lin whispered.

Mrs. Perkins fell back hard against the hallway wall. She clutched at her chest and her eyes rolled back in her head as she toppled to the floor, unconscious.

CHAPTER 25

Lin, Viv, Jeff, Anton, and Libby sat on the deck of John's boat eating appetizers, sipping drinks, and watching people stroll past on the docks. Nicky and Queenie sat together on the cushion of the built-in bench at the side of the deck. John was running late working with a real estate client so Viv promised to start the grilling for him. Because John was unaware of ghosts and Lin's ability to see them, discussion of such things had to halt when he was with the group so they took the opportunity to talk about what had happened at Mrs. Perkins's party.

As soon as the older woman had hit the floor, Lin pulled her phone out of her purse and placed the emergency call reporting Mrs. Perkins's collapse. Lin started CPR while shouting down the hall that they needed help, but no one heard her. The ambulance finally arrived and the young man who'd stood sentry at the lower level doors ushered the emergency personnel into the hallway where he stood proudly as if he had been the reason that the older woman survived the heart attack. Lin, dripping sweat from performing CPR for what seemed like an eternity, slumped against the wall as Mrs. Perkins was hauled away to the hospital.

Viv and Jeff rushed in and lifted Lin to her feet and as they helped her outside, she babbled about what had happened. "She knows what's behind the wall," Lin told them. "Her father must have confessed it to her." When they sat Lin down with a glass of water at one of the white café tables under the tent, she leaned forward and told Viv and Jeff that she knew what was behind the wall, too.

Enjoying the gentle sea breeze at the back of John's boat, Lin told the group, "I don't know how I knew, but I did."

Although Libby was still weak from the experience of seeing the vision of what had happened to William Weston, she wanted to get together with the others for an evening out and to share information that she'd gathered from her many contacts on the island. "Mrs. Perkins told the police that a few months before her father passed away, he confessed to her what he'd done. She didn't believe it and attributed his confession to his dementia. She didn't mention anything to the police or the hospital personnel about what Lin told her about the workmen or anything about ghosts or other such things ... which was a good thing or they may have questioned her mental state and committed her for observation."

Jeff told them what he'd heard from Kurt. "Kurt was called in by the police to remove the wall of the bedroom in the lower level of the mansion. The police were there when it was taken down. That's where they found the bones."

"I went to see Mrs. Perkins in the hospital." Lin brushed her hair back from her face. "She told me what her father had confessed to her. After they were married, Rowan Richards was abusive to Rose and she left him and moved to Boston where she ran into a smuggler from Rowan's gang. The man had run away from Nantucket, he'd had enough of the nasty business of the illegal smuggling. He knew what had happened to Rose's father and told Rose that Rowan had ordered her father to be killed so he wouldn't interfere with their relationship."

Lin continued, "Rose returned to Nantucket to confront Rowan. The two had a terrible fight and Rowan strangled Rose in the house. He buried her in the basement of the mansion and never told a soul what he'd done." Lin looked off towards the open sea for a few moments. "Mrs. Perkins asked me why those men had shown up in the lot recently. I told her that it might have been due to the renovations on the mansion, but that I didn't really know. She asked me if they would keep showing up. I said that I didn't think they would." Lin smiled. "Then she told me to leave her hospital room and if we ever ran into one another somewhere that I was to pretend that I'd never met her."

Viv scowled and said with sass, "I'm sure she thanked you for saving her life after she collapsed with a heart attack."

"She didn't." Lin shrugged.

Libby told the group that a few days ago, Rose Weston had been buried in the cemetery next to her father and mother. "May they now all rest in peace."

"John will be here soon." Viv got up to go below to get the burgers and veggie burgers to put them on the grill. She stopped at the top of the stairs and turned to Lin. "Have you seen William Weston since all the excitement?"

Lin shook her head.

"You will." Viv went down the stairs.

Jeff brought Lin an iced tea, kissed her head, and went below to help Viv bring up the food.

Anton pushed his glasses up his nose and sipped from his glass of wine. "Perhaps we'll have a peaceful last few weeks of August. Try not to see any more ghosts for a while, Carolin. Everyone needs a break."

Lin smiled and rolled her eyes at the historian. "I'll do my best."

"By the way, where is Leonard?" Anton asked. "I haven't seen him lately."

"He's been on the mainland for several days." Lin took a long drink from her glass. "After Mrs. Perkins was taken to the hospital and Jeff and Viv brought me outside, I noticed I had a text from Leonard." She smiled. "He told me to be careful at that party."

"That man has a very strong sense of intuition." Anton nodded.

John arrived at the boat looking dapper in a tan fitted suit grinning from ear to ear. "I sold that house over in Cisco." He wrapped Viv in a bear hug. "A huge commission is coming my way." John practically whooped as he went below to change into a polo shirt and shorts.

Everyone enjoyed the meal and spent the next couple of hours playing cards, chatting, and laughing with one another as the sun set and the stars came out to twinkle overhead in the dark night sky. The group reluctantly cleaned up and disbanded wishing a good night to all.

Jeff took Lin's hand and with the dog following along behind, they walked through the cozy streets of Nantucket town up the brick sidewalks under the streetlamps to the Civil War memorial where they took a left and continued their stroll to Lin's cottage. Even though Lin was pleased and grateful that Rose's body had been found and that William Weston could rest now, Lin's heart was heavy when she thought of the wickedness that humans could inflict on one another.

As they walked, Jeff talked about the work he had been doing on his own house in between all of the projects he had been working on for Kurt's company. Lin loved the way that Jeff took pride in every aspect of his craft and how he threw himself into everything he did. He was steady and kind and fun, and being with Jeff always made Lin feel safe and loved and valued. She looked up at him and smiled.

"What?" Jeff asked.

Lin grinned and shook her head, realizing that she had to focus on all the good there was in the world and that the man walking beside her was a whole lot of good. "Just thinking about how lucky I am."

"I spend a good part of my day thinking the very same thing."

Nicky gave a happy woof.

As Lin wrapped her arms around Jeff and rested her head against his chest, a whoosh of cold air swept over her and she shifted her eyes across the road.

With the atoms of their forms shimmering like diamonds, William Weston stood with his daughter, Rose, next to him and with a woman on the other side of Rose who Lin thought must be William's wife, Yvette. The three ghosts smiled at Lin, nodded, and then hand in hand, slowly turned to walk away. With her head still pressed against Jeff, Lin watched as the ghosts' particles sparkled and swirled, and then disappeared into the night air.

Lin took Jeff's hand and they continued their

walk down Vestry Road with the dog bouncing along ahead of them.

"Kurt has a new project. His team has been hired to work on an old lighthouse and he's asked me to join them. It's going to be interesting work. I was going to drive out there tomorrow and take a look, but I wondered if you'd like to bike there with me instead."

"That would be fun. I'd love to bike with you. We can pack a lunch and eat by the water. It would be nice to relax for a while. Which lighthouse is it?"

When Jeff told her, Lin felt a ping of something jump down her back. She decided to ignore it, knowing that whatever it was, it would find her if it needed to.

Until then, she was going to enjoy the rest of this perfect and lovely night.

THANK YOU FOR READING!

BOOKS BY J.A. WHITING CAN BE FOUND HERE:

www.amazon.com/author/jawhiting

To hear about new books and book sales, please sign up for my mailing list at:

www.jawhitingbooks.com

Your email will never be sold, shared, or spammed.

J.A Whiting

BOOKS BY J. A. WHITING

LIN COFFIN COZY MYSTERIES

A Haunted Murder (A Lin Coffin Cozy Mystery Book 1)
A Haunted Disappearance (A Lin Coffin Cozy Mystery Book 2)
The Haunted Bones (A Lin Coffin Cozy Mystery Book 3)
A Haunted Theft (A Lin Coffin Cozy Mystery Book 4)
A Haunted Invitation (A Lin Coffin Cozy Mystery Book 5)
The Haunted Lighthouse (A Lin Coffin Cozy Mystery Book 6) - soon
And more!

SWEET COVE COZY MYSTERIES

The Sweet Dreams Bake Shop (Sweet Cove Cozy Mystery Book 1)
Murder So Sweet (Sweet Cove Cozy Mystery Book 2)
Sweet Secrets (Sweet Cove Cozy Mystery Book 3)
Sweet Deceit (Sweet Cove Cozy Mystery Book 4)
Sweetness and Light (Sweet Cove Cozy Mystery Book 5)
Home Sweet Home (Sweet Cove Cozy Mystery

Book 6)
Sweet Fire and Stone (Sweet Cove Cozy Mystery Book 7)
Sweet Friend of Mine (Sweet Cove Cozy Mystery Book 8)
Sweet Hide and Seek (Sweet Cove Cozy Mystery Book 9) – soon!
And more!

OLIVIA MILLER MYSTERIES

The Killings (Olivia Miller Mystery Book 1)
Red Julie (Olivia Miller Mystery Book 2)
The Stone of Sadness (Olivia Miller Mystery Book 3)

If you enjoyed the book, please consider leaving a review.

A few words are all that's needed.

It would be very much appreciated.

ABOUT THE AUTHOR

J.A. Whiting lives with her family in New England. Whiting loves reading and writing mystery stories.

VISIT ME AT:

www.jawhitingbooks.com

www.facebook.com/jawhitingauthor

www.amazon.com/author/jawhiting

Printed in Great Britain
by Amazon